STRESS *Relief*

DIANA HUNTER

ELLORA'S CAVE
ROMANTICA PUBLISHING

An Ellora's Cave Romantica Publication

www.ellorascave.com

Stress Relief

ISBN 9781419961946
ALL RIGHTS RESERVED.
Stress Relief Copyright © 2009 Diana Hunter
Edited by Pamela Campbell.
Photography and cover art by Les Byerley.

Electronic book publication April 2009
Trade paperback publication 2010

STRESS RELIEF

જી

Prologue

ℰ

The whip fell across soft white shoulders that had never done hard lifting or heavy labor. These were shoulders used by friends to cry on, shoulders that pushed nothing stronger than a pen, shoulders that carried little more weight than that of a heavy wool coat in winter.

But now the whip cracked across their whiteness, leaving a trail of raised skin behind, forcing a cry of pain from the woman who hung by her wrists from chains. The woman who gave her shoulders to another to abuse...and excite.

Her head seesawed back and forth as a second crack raised another welt across her shoulder blades. The penis gag in her mouth gave her the freedom to scream as loudly as she wanted and she gave in to the urge, channeling the pain out of her body through the use of her voice. Her muffled cries came out as moans as a third stroke left its mark on her unblemished skin.

With her legs cuffed to a spreader bar that, in turn, fastened to the floor, keeping her balance was out of the question. So was keeping her sanity. When a fourth and fifth blow followed in quick succession, she threw her head back and howled, the pain forcing a catharsis of all her pent-up stress. Tears that never came easily coursed down her cheeks as her cries turned to sobs and the bottom of existence came up to hit her in the face.

All the troubles her friends had laid on her shoulders, all the issues with money, her parents' divorce, all the problems facing the world came pouring out of her soul. Barely aware that her legs had been released, Meg's heart poured out all the poison she'd held inside for far too long in salty tears that striped her cheeks, much like the stripes borne by her shoulders. Each crack of the rawhide whip pulled the pressures from her and when Jack released her wrists, she collapsed into the strength of his arms as he lowered her to the floor and held her tight.

Chapter One

ဨ

With a spring in her step that she hadn't felt in far too many months, Meg Tucker crossed the packed mall parking lot, heading to Coughlin's department store. In her position as buyer for women's dresses, she enjoyed being out in the stores, overseeing displays, talking with customers and personnel alike, to keep the operation moving smoothly.

The Saturday morning sun shone brightly today, giving her just a moment's hesitation as she stepped up onto the curb, the glass doors reflecting the brilliant blue sky of spring behind her. Days like this made her think twice about her chosen career. Never in high school would she ever have answered "Buyer" when asked what she wanted to be when she grew up. In fact, she rarely had an answer to that question back then. Not because she didn't know but because there were so many wonderful choices that she could never pick just one.

She'd worked as a cashier at Coughlin's through high school, then as a clerk in the women's department to help pay her way through college. She'd returned to the company after graduating with a BA in art...and no prospects. Old Mr. Coughlin himself had hired her as an assistant buyer. He'd told her that he liked his employees to have intelligence and that he'd provide the on-the-job training. That way he felt assured his people knew his methods and employees didn't have to unlearn "that nonsense passed out at the business schools today".

So Meg had lucked into a job fresh out of college that now, seven years later, it had become an ingrained habit. Deliberately pushing aside thoughts of a career as a painter and of turning her passion for gardening into a full-fledged

9

hobby, both provoked by the beautiful spring day, she set a smile on her face and continued along the sidewalk to the store's main entrance.

As she reached for the door, the fabric of her trim, navy blue business suit stretched across her shoulders. Even as her breath caught at the sudden ache, Meg fixed a smile on her face. That ache had been earned the hard way two days ago and she was darn proud of it. The release of tension the whipping had given her had been a long time coming—now her soul felt as light as a sunbeam.

That wonderful, walking-on-clouds feeling continued all morning and well into the afternoon. Nothing could touch her up here, nothing could bring her down or weigh her soul with stress. She beamed at everyone and everything.

A late afternoon double whammy of a customer complaint combined with a surly salesperson served as unwelcome reminders that Meg belonged on the earth, not in the sky, however. In spite of her best efforts to let the incidents slide off her flogged back, her smile didn't shine quite as brightly as she made her way back to her car after dinner, her stomach rumbling from one more skipped meal.

She had only a block to go, her upstairs apartment within sight, when the muffler on her car blew out. As she pulled away from the last light, a loud bang made her jump. She needed only seconds to realize the problem came from her own car. On any other day she might have sworn and thrown a magnificent hissy fit. But today she stubbornly clung to the remnants of her optimism while she drove the last few yards and maneuvered along the narrow driveway that barely fit between city houses built before the automobile had become so ubiquitous.

Parking in her allotted spot behind the two-family house, Meg took a moment to rub her tired eyes, deciding that the muffler could wait until morning. The relief she got from her sessions with Jack lasted less and less time. Making a mental note to let him know that, she headed up the stairs to her upper half of the house and to bed.

But bed would have to wait. A digital number blinked on her answering machine and Meg knew better than to ignore the two calls. She hit the button even as she multi-tasked, going through the mail, dropping the junk into the recycling bin tucked around the corner in the back bedroom she used for storage and setting the bills on the kitchen table as her mother's voice whined its way through a message.

"Megan, you really need to give me your cell phone number. I hate this damn machine. Your brother is ignoring me again. He's gone off with That Man.

"Call me as soon as you get home, Megan, dear. This house is so empty. You really don't need half a house all to yourself. I don't know why you don't just move home and save yourself the money. I know you're not making all that much and that way we'd both be company for each other."

The message clicked off, replaced by the machine's automated voice reporting the time of the call—a welcome change from her mother's nagging. Meg had good reasons for not giving her mother her cell phone number. And very good reasons why she would never move back home. Meg's smile dimmed a bit more as she checked the clock. She had half an hour before she really needed to return that call if she didn't want even more whining in her life. Idly, she slit open the bill envelopes as the second message kicked on.

"Meg, it's Jack. We need to talk. Something's come up. Call when you get in."

Alarmed, Meg grabbed for the phone. Jack did have her cell number. Why hadn't he used it if he needed her?

"Jack? Meg…what's up?"

"Meg…damn, this isn't a good time. Thought you'd be home earlier. My flight is boarding right now."

"Boarding? Flight? Where are you going?"

"Last minute…job I couldn't turn down…"

"Jack, your signal is breaking up...what are you talking about?"

"Sorry...call you later...Paris."

The line went dead and a headache started to pound in her temples.

* * * * *

The e-mail came the next morning.

Meg,

Got a chance to work with Roman Polanski. Yes! The Roman Polanski. Got the call from my agent at three and was on the plane for France by eight last night. Still can't believe it.

I'm sorry I'm not going to be there to experience your afterglow. I love how a good session makes you shine for an entire week. Again, sorry I left with so little warning but shooting starts in a few hours. Gotta love a business that goes from 0 to 160 in the space of a five-minute phone call.

Take care...hope you drank lots of water!

Jack

PS. This gig's a long one...twelve-week shoot on location. And I have the indie up next. Means another ten weeks after that. You're gonna need a new Dom. You've outgrown me anyway. Will e-mail you the names of some prospects later.

Meg slumped back in her desk chair, mostly happy for Jack. A pissed-off feeling nagged her though. She didn't want a new Dom. It had taken her long enough to find Jack. The last thing she wanted to have to do was break in a new one. She flexed her shoulders and shook her head. The welts had faded to thin, pink lines and the soreness diminished daily. She felt deflated, as though Jack had taken all her patience and good will with him on the plane, leaving her behind—stuck on the ground with all the stresses and frustration she'd hoped to be rid of for a much longer time.

The bright morning sun suddenly dodged behind a cloud and Meg shook her head, deciding that the rest of the office work she'd planned to finish today could wait. While she mostly liked her job, she also knew she wouldn't—couldn't— do it for the rest of her life. Working at Coughlin's was a job. Nothing more. Not a career and certainly not anything close to a vocation. That thought made her smile a little. Did anyone ever feel a calling to retail? She doubted it.

No, this job would do for now. But she had dreams that needed chasing too. Jack had flown across an entire ocean to follow his dream and Meg recognized the signs in herself that maybe her time was coming as well. Maybe the discontent she felt heralded a need for change? The thought gave her a little hope and made her feel a little less upset with Jack. Maybe he had a point.

A flash of lightning made her jump. Before the rumble of thunder echoed through her apartment, she started the shutdown process for her computer. As the heavens opened, she closed the window, then stood looking out over the tidy lawns of the upscale city neighborhood. For the past three years she'd rented this upper half of a house and loved the hominess of it.

"I'm becoming settled. That's the problem."

Turning from the window, she flipped on the TV and punched in the channel for the weather station. As she suspected, this was just a passing storm. She watched the dark green line of thunderstorms that moved from west to east, the yellow splotches showing the worst spots. A dark red button of thunderstorms hovered right over the northeast part of the city. As if to prove it, another bright flash made her jump, the thunder following almost immediately after.

Laughing at her own silliness, Meg idly flipped through the stations, watching snippets of Sunday-morning programming as the spring rain pelted against the windows. What was she going to do without a Dom? She and Jack weren't lovers, although sex usually made up part of their sessions. He wasn't really even in the "friends with benefits" category. He was her Dom. Period. The one she went to when she needed a good whipping. Meg chuckled as she remembered Jack telling her he was her "Father Confessor". Whenever her sins became too much to bear, he whipped them out of her along with all the stresses of life. She had to admit, he wasn't far off. The sins of her present rose like ghosts far too often.

The brash sound of the phone interrupted her reverie and Meg winced. Speaking of sins—she'd never called her mother last night. Now she was in for it. Tempted to just let it ring, she decided against it. Might as well pay the piper now than pay triple later.

"Hello?"

"Well, it's about time. Megan, didn't you get my message last night? Why didn't you call me back when you got home from work? Or are you telling me you finally had a date?"

Meg rolled her eyes. "No, Mom, no date. Came home exhausted and just went to bed, that's all."

"You work too hard at that dead-end job. No prospects, no advancement."

Her mother droned on and Meg stopped listening. She knew exactly what her mother meant by a lack of prospects, and she wasn't talking about the job. Nearly thirty, Meg felt perfectly happy without a permanent partner. Hadn't worked out real well for her parents, though her mother often overlooked that tiny little fact.

"Your brother is with That Man again. Honestly, after all he did to us, I cannot imagine why your brother wants to spend time with him."

"Mom, will you please stop referring to Dad as 'That Man'? Tom's always had a good relationship with Dad. I'd think you'd be glad for that."

"Glad? Glad?"

The last trace of good feelings from her recent flogging and her introspective debate disappeared. Holding her temper and barely listening to her mother, Meg fervently hoped Jack would find her a new Dom. Soon.

* * * * *

A long two days later, Meg found a terse note in her e-mail inbox:

Jack said you would be looking for a new Dom. If you're interested, read the attached and get back to me.

Rand Arthur

Awfully abrupt. Was this guy always like that? Or only when dealing with submissives? Maybe she was just jumping to conclusions. Jack knew her and her desires. He wouldn't tell just anybody to e-mail her.

The document attached read like a primer for beginning submissives. Neatly outlined were all the precautions that should be taken before meeting a new Dom, which put her into a slightly more generous frame of mind as she scrolled through the list, mentally ticking off the items. Meet in a public place first, have a cell phone and arrange for someone to call at specific intervals throughout that first meeting. Arrange a code word to use with the person on the other end of the phone in case you got scared and didn't want to say "help me" straight out. Alternately, have a friend go with you on the first visit.

Not a single new warning in the bunch but Meg kind of liked the fact that he'd attached the list. Showed he understood the real-life needs and fears that a sub would naturally feel at meeting someone for the first time. Meeting a new Dom wasn't a whole lot different than going out on a blind date. In both cases, much could go wrong, and having a way out? Imperative.

The second of the two documents seemed to have been written by a philosophy major. There he detailed a very explicit view of Dominance that actually followed along fairly closely with her own. He didn't want a girlfriend or any romantic entanglements, nor did he want a lover of any sort. All this guy looked for was a woman with whom he could relieve the pent-up stresses of daily life and have sex with. In short, he was perfect.

After alternately reading his treatise through a second time and pining for Jack's familiarity, Meg decided to trust Jack's recommendation. Before she could change her mind, she dashed off a reply, giving Rand several options for setting up that first meeting.

His answer came back within the hour and Meg agreed to meet him at a local ice cream stand at seven that evening. In a fit of whimsy, she told him she'd be the one with the spring flowers in her hair.

Of course, she wrote that before she examined the garden borders of her back yard. The landlord let her work off some of the rent by keeping the small gardens weeded and full. Cramped apartments were not her style. She wanted room to move around, to socialize, to play. This house suited her needs quite nicely and so far, she'd been lucky with the downstairs neighbors. The young couple who lived there now mostly kept to themselves and were often away. Meg grinned and wondered what Rand would say when he discovered she had several pieces of dungeon furniture in her spare bedroom.

As the sun moved toward nightfall, a sweet fragrance filled the garden. Meg paused, taking a deep breath to fully appreciate the heavy perfume of the Linden trees. Not many flowers bloomed in the beds right now but the quince and lilacs and azaleas were glorious. The buds on the property's lone rhododendron, however, clung stubbornly shut, not quite ready to reveal the delicate petals hiding inside. She smiled, glad she no longer felt that way about her sexual preferences. There was a time when, like the rhododendron, it took a lot of coaxing to expose herself, in more ways than one.

But that was before Jack. He'd taught her so much in the two years they'd been together. He'd been her tutor, her mentor in the glories of bondage and the various flower gardens that could be BDSM. The sweet flowers as well as the bitter ones…nothing was taboo with Jack.

But what about Rand? Meg wanted him to know she wasn't a shrinking violet. And she wasn't a delicate rose. Grinning, she decided she had more in common with the hardy mum. Dependable, weather resistant and tough.

But mums weren't in season. Cutting a sprig of lilac, she decided it could also work as a symbol for her. Feminine in color and fragrance, the flowers massed together to form a beautiful whole, just as her various parts worked together to create all that made up Meg Tucker. Still feeling jaunty, she pulled her hair into a ponytail, stuck the sprig into the band and headed out for ice cream.

Chapter Two

❧

Rand Arthur knew Meg as soon as she got out of the little runabout car. In his hurried phone call, Jack had waxed poetic over the woman's "soft brown hair" and "eyes like a doe" and Rand had harrumphed in skepticism. Closest Jack Williams had ever been to a doe was watching *Bambi*. Rand had accused his fellow Master of going soft on a girl but that had been emphatically denied. Jack insisted Meg was really more of a student of his, a student in the world of BDSM. When Jack admitted he'd gone off to Europe with hardly a goodbye to the woman, Rand had decided he must be telling the truth. Meg simply played bottom to Jack's top. Now Rand needed to decide if he wanted her for his own sexual use.

Sitting in the cab of his pickup, he formed his own impressions of her, noting the roundness of her face, the darkness of her hair—currently pulled into a tidy ponytail— the jaunty way she scanned the crowd, looking for him. He remained in his truck, watching her, studying the way she moved and how she stood—totally at ease, not showing a trace of nervousness at meeting him.

Not plump but not skinny either. She had a bit of meat on her bones, as his uncle used to say. Rand liked that. He hated women who were nothing but muscle and sinew. He knew his preferences were not currently popular but he liked women who felt soft and smelled nice.

Meg turned away and Rand smiled to see the lavender-colored bloom nestled in her dark tresses. Jack definitely had good taste. Making a decision, he opened the door and unfolded his tall frame from the truck's cab. Coming up softly behind her, he discovered he didn't need to bend very far to whisper in her ear. Jack hadn't mentioned her height and Rand was pleasantly surprised to discover she wasn't much shorter than his own six-foot-three. Wanting to see if he could mentally throw her, he whispered, "With thirty-some odd flavors at your command, tell me your choice."

Meg didn't jump but he felt her stiffen a moment in surprise before a slow smile spread across her face as she turned toward him. Whatever answer she was going to give him, however, remained unsaid as her eyes, all set to look down, turned upward instead. Her smile became a grin and Rand noted how her eyes crinkled at the corners when it did.

"Jack didn't tell me you were taller than me."

"I suspect he didn't tell us a lot of things, Ms. Tucker."

She considered a moment, then gave a little toss of her head. "Good." Her eyes gave him the once over and Rand felt confident that she would not find him wanting. It was only fair—he'd already looked his fill before she knew he was there. Of course, that study hadn't told him how sexy her voice could be—a deep alto that promised nights of silk and leather rather than nights of satin and lace.

"In my ice cream—and only in ice cream—I like vanilla."

She could even make such a plain choice sound sensuous. He smiled and took the liberty of pushing back a small lock of hair that had fallen from the ponytail. "And why do you like vanilla in your ice cream, Meg Tucker?"

The use of her name unnerved her a little, just as he hoped it would. People weren't used to others using their full name. Science and technology may have progressed but names still held power, a power he loved to wield.

"Simple flavors are deceptive. They form a solid base to build upon. Add chocolate syrup and peanuts and you have a sundae. Or slices of banana and whipped cream for a split. Each addition creates something new. Something it could never have been without the solid, simple base, Rand Arthur."

She used his name right back at him, playing his own game. And she didn't fool him. Ice cream was not what she was talking about. Enjoying her wit, he continued the discussion. "And do you have a preference between splits and sundaes? Or even shakes?"

Meg shook her head. "I like them all. Variety is what makes life interesting, don't you think?" With another grin, she turned and stepped into the short line. Definitely intrigued, Rand stood behind her, noting how the top of her head came just above his mouth. The perfume of the lilac in her hair filled his nose and he breathed deeply.

"I think variety is exactly what you're going to get, young lady."

Too many ears were close and Rand wouldn't discuss the particulars of what they both wanted while still in the hearing distance of children. They ordered their cones, vanilla for her and a soft twist of chocolate and vanilla for him, and by an unspoken agreement, wandered away from the bright lights of the ice cream stand toward the park that stretched off into the darkness behind it. Staying on the well-worn path, they walked side-by-side down to the river and the wide dock that jutted into the waterway. One other couple already leaned on the rail overlooking the moonlit water but it was pretty obvious they were not even aware that he and Meg had joined them. Nodding to the opposite side of the dock, Rand leaned against the rail and continued his study of the woman beside him.

Meg knew he measured her fitness as a sub. Keeping her face neutral, she let him look, while mentally evaluating him as well. Used to being taller than most men she knew, his height made her feel more feminine. Dark hair that held no curls, cut short but not too short. No military discipline here, yet she couldn't deny he held her attention. He moved with an authority seen in men who were used to people doing their bidding. She watched his hands as he held and licked the ice cream cone that threatened to melt on his fingers, unable to tell if they were callused but their power certainly was evident.

With his shirtsleeves rolled to his elbows, she got a good look at his muscles, just as she suspected he meant her to.

In fact, there wasn't one thing he'd shown her that she wasn't meant to see, she realized. He already controlled the amount of information he gave her, determining where they walked, even how they stood. He leaned back in comfort against the rail while she stood beside him, the moonlight revealing her face. She tipped her cone to him in silent acknowledgement of a game well played.

"So what are you looking for in a bottom?" she asked.

He stared off into the distance as though thinking it over, yet when he replied, the words came with an ease that told her he'd already spent years considering this question.

"Someone who isn't afraid of emotional travel. Someone who understands there are places she can't go alone, that I can't go alone. It's a journey only two people can take and only if one leads and the other follows. An independent someone. Not a person I have to mollycoddle in any way. A woman who can stand on her own two feet and make all her own decisions yet who is willing to put her hand in mine and travel a road open to us only if we journey together." He looked over at her as if in challenge. "And what are you looking for in a Top?"

Meg smiled and her face softened. "Someone who can handle my passions. Someone who understands that pain and pleasure are closely linked and who isn't afraid to explore the fluid edges between them. Someone I can give my trust to."

"Trust takes time to build."

Meg nodded. "We've already taken several steps in that direction, to borrow your metaphor. First, Jack recommended you and I trust him without reservation. Second, you were on time tonight." She smiled at his look of surprise. "I saw you in the truck as I pulled into the parking lot. Was curious as to how you'd approach me, though, so I pretended I didn't. I apologize for that. Should we take this further, that's the last time I'll pretend with you."

Rand's appraisal of the woman beside him rose considerably. Very few women, in his experience, had the presence of mind that Meg exhibited. She just might prove to be an interesting partner. "Good. I want total honesty. The trust goes both ways. I need to be able to trust you to tell me the truth, both when we're in a scene and when we're just talking."

"So it seems we're already on this journey together."

"It would appear that we are."

Meg shifted, turning around to lean against the rail as she finished off the rest of her cone. The breeze brushed against her face and she reached up to pull out her ponytail. Her fingers found the lilac and she held it in one hand as her other released her long hair to fall past her shoulders and down along her back. Not quite to her waist, the straight dark brown hair lifted in the wind and danced behind her.

Rand reached over and took the flower from her fingers, lifting it to savor the scent before turning and throwing it into the river with a flourish. Meg spun and watched it float away, turning and twisting as the current took it.

"Are you prepared to be the flower, Meg? To be controlled by someone else's whims and fancies? To be pushed and pulled along a current you can't see?" He leaned in and dropped his voice so only she could hear his question. "Are you prepared to trust me?"

Meg's stomach gave a little flip, a feeling she'd not had in a very long time. Flirting with Rand meant flirting with danger and it excited her. A lot. Heat came up in her cheeks as her heartbeat quickened. Taking a deep breath to steady herself, she looked for the calm within. Finding it, she pushed off from against the rail and stood to face him. "I am."

Rand nodded and also straightened. "I am also prepared to trust you, Meg." He liked how her eyes flashed when he called her by name. This one wore her emotions very close to the surface. She would be refreshing indeed. "But not tonight.

Tonight is for first meetings, for finding the right wave to ride, if you will. If you're available tomorrow night, we can both ride this wave into shore and see if we've ended up in the same place."

Meg dropped her eyes to cover the small disappointment she felt at not playing with him right now. She came back ready with a tease, however. "You certainly are one for metaphors. Must be your poetic soul."

He did not smile. "Creating a scene requires a certain sense of the poetic, don't you agree?"

Chastened, Meg nodded, once again dropping her eyes. He was right, of course. Damn. She knew that too. Jack's incredible ability to set a scene was one of the reasons she had continued to play with him long after she'd outgrown the role of student. He had a way of crafting an experience that never failed to give her one heck of a ride. Looking at Rand now, Meg realized the scenes her new Dom crafted would look very different from what she was used to and yet be well worth her time.

"You understand I'm only in this for the relief of tension," she told him, wanting to be very clear about her motives.

"Then our motives are the same. Nothing gets rid of stress better than giving someone a good whipping." He dropped his voice. "Whether they deserve it or not."

Again Meg felt a powerful surge of attraction that made her pussy cream. Rand had gestured to the path that would take them back to their respective cars and as she climbed the small hill, she realized that attraction was a good thing. She didn't need romance in her life right now and a boyfriend would only be a drag on her time. But finding an attractive Dom who could easily become a friend was something she'd never expected to find twice in her life.

Rand opened her car door for her and Meg paused before sliding in. "What time tomorrow night shall I see you? And where?"

"We're still building trust. Here's my card." He pulled out a business card with a practiced fluidity and scribbled an address on it before handing it to her. "Do you like Chinese food?"

"Very much." Meg accepted his card, not yet glancing at it.

"Meet me at The Golden Duck at six o'clock. We'll have a light dinner. This way we'll both have another opportunity to back out before we get in too deep."

Meg had already made up her mind—was Rand having second thoughts? She chewed her lip and turned the card over in her hand. The open door separated them but as Rand stepped forward and took her chin in his fingers, the air practically shimmered between them.

"Trust me."

She looked up into his dark blue eyes, now lit only by the yellow neon light that ringed the ice cream stand. Calm assurance and quiet confidence radiated from him. Meg nodded. "All right, I will."

He bent down and kissed her upturned face—a small goodnight kiss. He didn't ask permission, he didn't waver or hesitate. He simply leaned down and caught her lips with his, his tongue pressing gently but insistently against them until she relented and opened for him. But once she'd given way, he didn't press his advantage, content to have persuaded her to relinquish power. In short, Rand gave her a taste of what his dominance would be like.

And as she drove home, the taste of his kiss still on her lips, Meg decided she needed to send Jack a thank you note.

Chapter Three

ஐ

The store clerk looked up as the small bell rang over the door, his breath catching in his throat at the rugged-looking customer sauntering into this off-the-beaten path kink store. The man held a ruggedness so imposing that, without saying a word, he sucked all attention to him simply by entering. With the customer's dark brown hair, cut to a length just long enough to be silky, and blue eyes that flashed as they found the case of floggers, the clerk's attention was immediate. The man wore jeans and cowboy boots as if he'd been born into a saddle, yet none of the air of the lonesome cowboy surrounded this one. The shirtsleeves on his plain blue shirt were rolled up, giving a glimpse of strong arms the clerk knew could crush him. He stifled a sigh and went to wait on the gorgeous hunk, praying that the customer would turn out to be gay.

Rand Arthur felt the young buck's appreciation and ignored it, trying to remain focused on his purpose for patronizing this particular store. The e-mail from Jack kept nagging at the back of his mind, however, as he tried to figure out just what his friend was plotting. Jack had sent women Rand's way in the past but this e-mail had been oddly worded. *Take care of her, Rand. This is the one you've been looking for. I've trained her just for you.* What the hell did his fellow Dom mean by that? Still, Meg intrigued him and with her in mind, he'd come out shopping today. He had dwelt on the soft curves of her ass for quite a while last night and he wanted to find just the right instrument to turn her skin a bright pink should she prove to be worthy of more of his time.

Rand held no misconceptions about that part. While they both retained the power to walk away after that first meeting, no questions asked, he already knew what his answer would be should she give him approval. The ball lay in her court at the moment but the second she volleyed it back to him, he wanted to be ready.

The clerk, still giving Rand a blushing once-over, handed over the item he'd indicated. Hefting the black leather flogger, Rand weighed it, balancing the instrument over his palm. Taking a step back from the counter and checking to see that he had enough room in the leather goods store, he raised it over his head in twirls that picked up speed as he tested it against the wind.

"No, not right." He didn't even need to slap it against the dressmaker's dummy that was so thoughtfully provided by the shop. The thongs dragged on this one. "Heft is right, thongs are too stiff."

The clerk gave Rand a slow smile, nodding his agreement. "I like a softer thong myself. Something to caress rather than sting." Flashing a small smile and a coy look, the male clerk returned the ill-made flogger to its spot under the glass.

Having now determined that the broad-shouldered man knew the difference between tools that were barely usable and tools that were true works of art, the clerk opened a small cupboard behind him and took out a long cardboard tube. "This, I think, is more your style." He slid the cloth-covered contents onto the glass-topped counter, then slowly peeled back the soft fabric to reveal the deer hide flogger that nestled inside.

Rand recognized the quality at once. The supple thongs were not simply knotted onto the handle, or worse, stapled. Each of these tan strips of suede wove around the handle in an intricate pattern of diamonds, making a fitting metaphor for the intertwining of the Dominant and submissive relationship. He lifted the heavy flogger from the counter, feeling the deceptive softness in the handle that hid a hard block of wood under the weaving.

This was not a flogger to wheel overhead, though. This beauty had been designed for an entirely different purpose.

Rand let the loose ends fall over his forearm, watching the slow cascade of the thongs, each a uniform finger-width wide. This was a flogger designed to just brush the skin, to plant kisses of passion with each stroke. A slightly stronger slap would leave deep blossoms of warmth, but an intense strike? With a sudden movement, he pivoted toward the dummy and landed a hard blow across the fabric-covered breasts.

Behind the counter, the clerk jumped, his cock rising at the sight of such superior power. The dummy wobbled a little on its single pole but neither he nor the customer paid any attention. "You need a better surface than that old thing if you want to know what it truly does," he murmured.

"Then take off your shirt and let me test its limits."

Steel eyes commanded him. His cock at full attention now, the buck stepped from behind the counter, pulling off his T-shirt as he went. He didn't need to be told twice. With total submission, he stood before a display of magazines. Leaning his palms against the wall for support, he dropped his head and presented his bare shoulders to the customer's mercy.

Rand had sized up the boy as soon as he'd entered the shop. He'd seen the little smiles and heard the invitation in his voice. It wasn't difficult to figure out what the kid was thinking. Rand's eyes narrowed, judging his age to be mid- to late twenties. About ten years younger than himself. While Rand preferred the company of women, he didn't mind taking—or giving—a little pleasure whenever the opportunity arose. And to judge by the bulge in the clerk's pants, it had arisen.

The flogger's handle fit his large palm perfectly. Standing a few feet behind the waiting back, Rand swung his arm out to the side several times, getting used to the weight and the way the thongs fell. He grinned as a shadow crossed the magazine rack and he looked out the storefront window at the person passing by. Even though the street didn't get much pedestrian traffic, the thought that someone might walk in gave the test an air of dangerous excitement.

Rand swung, letting the thongs brush air past the boy's back, enjoying the way he flinched away from a blow that didn't fall. But blows were not really what this instrument was about. This leather was designed to caress the skin, awaken it. Rand swung again, letting the thongs, heavy with sensuous sexuality, stroke the young man's naked skin.

The kid's head dropped down as Rand increased the tempo, the tips of the thongs massaging the shoulders into relaxing. Attuning himself to the boy's reactions, Rand watched for the rise and fall of those shoulders that would signal the settlement of the mind into an open, submissive state.

Shifting the flogger to his left hand, Rand changed the tempo and force again, swiping sideways and letting the thongs wrap around the submissive's body in a temporary leather hug. A moan and a movement told him the boy needed relief. He paused, then gave a command, pushing himself as well as his temporary sub.

"Your pants are in the way of my giving you the flogging you need. Take them off."

Without hesitation, the skinny clerk unzipped his jeans and dropped them to the floor. He wore no underwear, a fact that didn't surprise Rand at all. "As the leather commands your body, I give you permission to come. Choose a magazine to receive you."

To no one's surprise, the kid chose a glossy magazine geared toward leathermen. The well-built model on the cover, his muscled chest flexed and buff, stood with his thumbs in the waistband of his jeans, pulling down the fabric to draw attention to his well-endowed cock. The clerk stuck it in the rack right in front of his own cock, a slender rod that nonetheless stood hard and powerful. Keeping one hand on the wall for balance and the other already working his cock, the clerk nodded and Rand resumed.

"Come when you are ready."

He rained the blows of the flogger harder now, truly putting the piece of equipment to the test. The suede thongs turned the skin from pink to red yet did not raise welts or cut the skin. Rand nodded. This was indeed a wonderful instrument. He'd been looking for something a bit more forceful when he'd come in but this little toy would make a very nice addition to his collection.

The buck's mind reeled as his skin burned under the constant assault. The pressure built inside him—a stranger seeing him naked, being used as an object for the express purpose of trying out a new flogger and no other reason, the thrill of doing it in the shop, in full view of anyone who passed by or who walked in. With a cry of blessed relief, he came on the cover of the magazine he'd chosen. White cum spurted out and soaked the model's face and chest. He continued to pump his cock as the flogger's dance on his back slowed, not stopping until he could no longer see the model for the cum that covered him.

"Clean yourself up and then come back and ring this up. I'll take it."

Unable to speak, the clerk nodded, taking the magazine with him to the back room. A small bathroom off the office in the back was sufficient for him to wash up and put his pants back on. The shirt he'd left behind the counter and with a huge grin on his face, he went out to retrieve it.

The customer didn't ask for a discount and the clerk didn't offer one. The fact that this had been strictly a business affair would serve as fuel for several more masturbations. He watched as the customer tucked the flogger, wrapped in its protective cloth and slipped back into the cardboard tube, under his arm and sauntered casually out the door. Whoever ended up on the receiving end of that thing in the future was one lucky son of a bitch. The clerk smiled as he pulled his shirt back on. At least he had the pleasure of knowing it had been used on him first.

* * * * *

Dinner later that night at The Golden Duck consisted solely of a shared pu-pu platter. "I'd rather play with you when your stomach isn't full. Getting to know your body will be a wonderful adventure and I'd like to keep it that way," Rand explained. Meg didn't mind and in fact, only picked at the platter, letting him eat the lion's share of the treats. She considered not eating anything. The first session with a new Dom always made her nervous. They could talk about trust until the end of time but only after she was tied up and totally helpless would she find out the truth. And by then it could be too late.

Rand held the door for her as they left. "So we've met for ice cream and a short date. You still have an opportunity to back out before we head back to my house and a session."

Meg shook her head. "I'm fine. Nervous, but fine."

Thank goodness his eyes twinkled or she might have balked at the deep, evil tone he affected. "Good. Follow me. I'll be sure not to lose you."

Sliding into traffic behind his truck, Meg took the opportunity to take a good look at the vehicle he drove. Definitely a newer model but the dings and scratches on the tailgate told her Rand used the truck more for adventures than as a showpiece model for appearance's sake. The camper top over the back boasted one cracked window on the side where it looked like something had hit against the safety glass. She compared his truck to her own second-hand, two-door, manual transmission runabout that served her needs, deciding that they both seemed to prefer the serviceable over the status symbol.

She threw her car into overdrive as they sped up the ramp to the expressway, glad she had a modicum of control in driving herself to their session. Having her car right outside his house gave her a small feeling of security that she could escape quickly if need be. Meg chose to ignore the fact that it was quite possible she'd never escape at all.

She knew from his card that he owned an investment firm with an office in a very respectable suburb. While her own career in retail had taken her partway up the ladder of financial success, she certainly hadn't reached the height he had achieved.

Meg followed Rand through the streets of the city and out into the ritzy suburb where all the city's big shots lived, wondering how her artsy friend Jack had ever met this guy in the first place. Following Rand, she turned off the street and into a gated drive that circled in front of the house. The sprawling Tudor surrounded by immaculate gardens oozed money. She grinned. A lot different from playing with Jack in his loft. In fact, the lack of privacy there was one of the reasons she'd begun setting up her own dungeon. A dungeon she now saw as small and unimpressive compared to what must lie behind those leaded-glass windows and dark wood trims.

She sat back in her seat and watched him get out of his truck, every movement a study in control. He intrigued her. Owned his own company, lived in a house just one step down from a mansion, yet he drove a truck designed for hauling. Others noticed him simply because he existed. She'd seen that in the restaurant when the maître d' had practically fallen over himself to seat them and the waitress blushed every time she approached the table. Rand Arthur didn't need to pose and posture like so many other men who fancied themselves Masters and Doms. Rand Arthur embodied what all those poseurs aspired to be.

And very shortly, he would turn all that concentrated power on her. Meg took a deep breath, letting it out slowly and closing her eyes to begin centering herself for what lay ahead. When she opened them again, the barely suppressed excitement of the game they were about to begin shone in her eyes.

Rand waited beside his truck, watching Meg take in her surroundings and adjust her mental state, finding himself more than a little attracted to the woman who now emerged, unfolding from her little car like a butterfly from a cocoon. He'd done some checking—just to make sure she wasn't the type to beg in the bedroom and cry rape in the streets. Besides Jack's recommendation, which certainly held a lot of weight, Rand found out she'd been with Coughlin's for just over ten years, working herself up from running the register to running the department. From his own conversations with her, he knew Meg Tucker had a good wit, was certainly a looker and loved kinky sex. And she ran from commitments in life as fast as he did. In short? The perfect playmate.

Rand didn't move as she approached, her gaze sweeping the expanse of yard and garden in curiosity and interest.

"Nice gardens," she commented as she came to stand beside him, her attitude seemingly relaxed. But the way her hands flitted, not staying still as they talked, told a different story. She was still nervous. And she was stalling.

"The company I use does a good job."

He discovered she could raise an eyebrow. "Company? You don't get out and get dirty yourself?"

"Used to. Like to haul and plant and mow my own lawn. But life keeps me too busy to do as much as I'd like and still keep the place up for appearances. Only the vegetable garden out back is all mine now."

He didn't ask if she wanted to take a look, even though the garden held high honor as one of his prides in life. Maybe someday but right now he had other activities on his mind. His cock stirred at the thought of tying this one down, playing with her body until she begged him to stop, then fucking her silly, all while she lay bound and helpless before him.

"You remember your safeword?"

"Yes…potato."

"And the gesture?"

"Left fist balled, thumb and pointer out."

"This way."

He led her into the house, not really giving her time to look around as he led her though a labyrinth of hallways and rooms off rooms, each step taking them farther from the public part of the house. Situated on a slope of land, one didn't need to go up or down stairs in order to go underground. After several twists and turns, Rand stopped before a heavy wooden door with an ornate grillwork covering a small, amber glass window. He'd had the door specially designed to resemble a door more commonly found as a front door. The grillwork contained figures, however, that evoked a feeling of warning rather than welcome. Demons intertwined with cherubs, captured for all time in positions of sexual ecstasy. He pulled a key from his pocket and unlocked the heavy door, watching her reaction as he did so.

To her credit, she didn't hesitate to cross the threshold. In fact, she did so almost eagerly.

The walls of beige concrete radiated coolness. Recessed lighting along the high ceiling cast a soft light, revealing a large room with several items of bondage furniture spaced widely apart. Sconces on the walls lent a more medieval appearance. The swept flagstone floor gave the room an austere quality, except for one corner set off from the rest of the room by a plush oriental rug and several large cushions. A slight chill in the air gave her the distinct impression that their travels through the house had led them deep under the hill, an impression made stronger when she realized the large room contained no windows that could spill the secrets within. And once Rand shut the heavy door, Meg realized sound would not escape either.

She stood awkwardly, suddenly unsure of procedure. Each Dom had his own way of starting scenes...and when she thought about it, Rand had already begun this scene, first back in the restaurant as he further probed her philosophy and then here in the house by leading her so quickly that she became disoriented and confused by the layout of the rooms. Now that they'd reached their destination, however, she wasn't sure of what he expected from her.

As if he sensed her unease, Rand gestured for her to stand beside him near a small electronic console. Taking another deep breath, she held it a moment before exhaling slowly and calming her thoughts. The soft strains of a Celtic flute filled the room and she smiled.

He didn't touch her right away, nor did he speak. Instead, she watched as he followed his own mental process to center himself, leaving the world outside the thick door. She listened to the music that floated around them, grounding her thoughts and opening her mind to his domination, suspecting Rand's mental process followed much the same path.

For several moments, he closed his eyes and Meg could almost see the energy flow into him in its own time, each passing second giving more and more strength to his will and to his mind and to his body. And when the music grew and the power filled him to bursting, he opened his eyes and turned that strength on her.

Meg watched Rand's transformation from just a normal guy, confident in his own abilities, to a powerful man clad in authority. His eyes gleamed with controlled desires. He could devour her...and would do so gladly. His shoulders seemed more squared, his chin more set. Her heart beat hard to think this man might be able to control the passions that so often ran rampant in her mind and soul.

"You are still wearing clothes."

The words were harsh, commanding, even though a command hadn't been given. He almost sounded displeased. Meg didn't budge. He held the power but she still wanted him to prove he deserved to wield it. She raised her chin a bit more as she looked into his eyes, trying to read their depths. "Do you have a command for me?"

A small glimmer of amusement flickered in his eyes. "Remain still while I undress you."

She nodded and his fingers came forward to unbutton her blouse. His eyes didn't leave hers, however, and Meg found his scrutiny a little unnerving even as he slowly uncovered her body to his view. When his fingers brushed her shoulders as he pushed the blouse off, she blushed even as she moved to let the sleeves slide past her hands. He took her blouse and draped it over a chair behind him as the music shifted to a sensuous alto sax pealing out a slow blues melody.

Scenes with Jack had become formulaic, she now realized, as Rand bid her turn with a circular motion of his finger. Jack had preferred for her to undress outside the playroom and enter naked and ready to play. Rand took his time, peeling her clothes off by layers, while at the same time peeling off her emotional layers as well. Not knowing his style, she'd worn a sexy blouse and skirt that could be removed easily and quickly.

Meg felt the heat of Rand's body as he stood behind her, his hands on her waist. Barely breathing, she remained still as a statue as he unzipped her skirt and let it fall. With the season turning warmer, she hadn't bothered with stockings, so all that remained were her high-heeled sandals, her bra and her thong.

Rand went for the underwear next but instead of removing the thin thong, he grabbed the back and pulled it up hard against her pussy and ass, forcing a surprised gasp out of her as she rose onto her tiptoes. "I like seeing you dance like this," he murmured in her ear, pulling the thin scrap of fabric up tighter. She shifted from foot to foot trying not to fall over, her hand reaching to find stability by grabbing his forearm.

But he didn't want her balanced just yet. He and Jack had Dommed together in the past and Rand knew Jack's style lay on the sensuous side, moving from a slow buildup to a fantastic climax. From what Jack had mentioned in his e-mail, Meg would expect the same type of buildup from Rand. Except that wasn't his style at all.

Rand shook off her hand, dropped his grip, quickly unsnapped her bra and pushed it roughly off her shoulders and down her arms. She struggled a little, unbalanced. He propelled her around so that she faced him, still on her toes, knowing her mind suddenly whirled at his rough treatment. He grabbed her arms and pulled her toward him, her face an inch away, her eyes almost level with his. "You will dance to my tune tonight. You are nothing more than my puppet."

The music shifted to a more lively beat, almost sprightly. Turning her again, Rand pulled her across the floor to a set of chains that hung in neat, parallel lines of silver. A wide, hard cuff dangled at the end of each of the four chains, just waiting for the wrists and ankles of the submissive in his hands.

Rand had her wrist locked into a cuff before Meg fully recovered from his sudden violence. The music blared now, the melody wildly careening in circles that made her dizzy. Even as she tested the binding, trying to pull her hand through the small opening, Rand fastened the other, stretching her arms out to the sides.

The remaining two chains hung almost to the floor and as the music reached a crescendo, he buckled her ankles into their cuffs, forcing her legs apart so she stood like a giant star.

Sudden silence filled the room, a silence that threatened to deafen her. Meg's heartbeat slowed as Rand watched her, a fierce light burning in his eyes. She swallowed several times as her mind adjusted to her new position. He had bound her so quickly, the event happening so fast, that it took several moments for her to realize escape was now impossible.

He just stood there, his arms crossed against his chest, eyes narrowed as if waiting for her to cry out. She wasn't about to give him the satisfaction. The thong she still wore rubbed along her slit, soaked with her cream, and Meg realized she had never been so turned on in her life. If she could only close her legs, she'd be able to come right here, right now. But the chains prevented that and her arousal hung as suspended as she.

With a motion almost too quick for her eye to follow, Rand snapped something out of his pocket, his fingers twirling first one way and then the other. In seconds, a switchblade gleamed in his hand, the steel sharp and pointed. Okay, this wasn't funny. She suddenly realized all she didn't know about this guy. Yeah, Jack had recommended him but what else did she really know except that he ate chocolate and vanilla twist ice cream cones, owned his own company and lived in a gorgeous house? Meg fought panic as Rand approached, the blade held out to his side, ready for use. In spite of her decision not to cry out, a whimper escaped and she knew he saw her fear.

"This is in the way of my enjoyment." Roughness edged his voice as his free hand closed on the front of her thong, pulling it forward, hard against her sensitive skin. Her ass burned anew and her clit throbbed despite her concerns. "Don't move. The blade is sharp."

Meg took shallow breaths and tried not to dance on her toes as he pulled her off balance once more. Instinct brought her arms forward to grab onto his shoulders but the chains prevented her from doing anything more than waving her arms a few inches forward and back. Even her feet wouldn't—couldn't—cooperate. She could only lift one leg at a time and balance on the toes of the other.

Rand waited until she stopped floundering about. With the way he'd hung her she couldn't fall, even though he had planned it so she would think otherwise. He could smell the fear and arousal on her and it settled into the core of his power, feeding him.

Satisfied that the woman had found her balance, he couldn't resist playing with her mind. Knowing she couldn't see the blade, he turned the handle to run along her hip, the cold metal sending a shiver of fear.

Her reaction was predictable, yet satisfying. She pulled away, crying out, "No!"

Rand kept hold of her panties and warned her again. "If you want me to cut you, by all means, pull away." He yanked her back into position and leaned in close to her face. "Stay still."

She nodded, unable to look at him. Good. He wanted her afraid of him. Fear and excitement were closely linked. In time she would come to trust him and that fear would no longer exist. But for now, he intended to enjoy every moment of terror in her eyes. With a flourish, he cut through the fabric of her panties in one fluid cut to the left and another to the right. The thin straps fell away, leaving only the scrap that he held onto—buried tight in her pussy. He grinned as he flipped the switchblade closed and slowly pulled the fabric toward him, knowing the thong rubbed against her ass, pussy and clit all at the same time.

The cry came as the thong pulled free. She hovered so close to coming he knew her mind was filled with it. Her eyes, which had closed as the fabric pushed her closer to the brink, now flew open at the sudden loss and her right foot slammed to the floor in a clink of metal as once more he threw her off balance.

Rand stepped close to her sweating body, enjoying the sheen of her skin. But he hadn't finished tormenting her mind. He whispered only two words before stepping away.

"My puppet."

Designing and building this machine had taken him the better part of six months and Rand had loved every moment of it. This was the first time he'd control a live person with it, however. His previous sub had found another Master before he finished and Rand had been too busy since she'd left to look for another. If it hadn't been for Jack's pleading phone call and intriguing e-mails, he wouldn't even be here now, trying out his new machine on a new sub and testing her possibilities.

Rand felt confident that Meg hadn't looked up and seen what hung over her head. That series of cables and pulleys connected to the central controls he'd shown her when they first entered. From there he could dictate the music, the lighting...and Meg.

Rand stepped behind her and out of her vision. She didn't have time to wonder what new torment he planned as a whirring over Meg's head made her look up at the same time that her right arm moved forward and down, pulled by the cuff around her wrist. Her attention snapped to her moving arm, for a moment not comprehending. Even as she watched her right arm, her left rose up at the same time that her right leg slid up and forward in a giant step. From behind her, she heard Rand repeat the words that sent shivers down her spine.

"My puppet."

Her cheeks burned as he lifted her arms and legs in a jerky dance. When he pulled her wrists above her head and then released them, she fought for control. But then he pulled a leg out from under her and her attention scattered as he drove home the fact that her body moved only according to his will. Incoherent squeals and protests came out of her mouth as her mind tried to deal with the ever-changing positions of her body.

She got both legs under her again, only to have her hands come down to the level of her breasts. But if he wanted her to feel herself, she wasn't about to comply. Not entirely sure that this was fun, she watched her right hand drop lower, close to her body. She balled her fist, deliberately not fingering herself. His chuckle from behind took the victory away.

Once again, he raised first one leg and then the other, only this time he didn't return them to the floor, leaving her suspended in a V, her legs spread wide, about a foot above her head. He brought her arms together and she could feel the muscles in her shoulders and back strain as they held her weight and she realized why the stiff cuffs had supports built into them.

Originally, Rand had used the traditional ropes to make a puppet, standing above the dummy he experimented with and pulling on each limb manually. But the cinch he used to fasten the ropes had to be mounted on the wall too far away and took too much time to fasten down. Playing with his marionette was the fun part. Using chains for strength and adding in a series of motors and pulleys had come close and with the addition of a series of tracks in the ceiling, Rand had decided that he'd created the perfect puppet machine.

And Meg certainly seemed to be the perfect woman to try this contraption out on. She squealed and protested at all the right times, fighting him and putting the machine through its paces. He enjoyed her resistance. Gave him something to work with. She might have given him her body to play with but he had to earn the right to control her mind.

Deliberately taking his time, he stepped around the control panel to stand beside his new submissive. He'd positioned her with her back about four feet off the ground and her legs spread wide, higher than that. Her head hung back, despite her efforts to keep it raised. Making note of the tension in her arms, he understood she wouldn't be able to hold the position long. This time.

Ostensibly taking pity on her, he bent down and put his hand under her head in support so he could talk with her a moment. "My puppet," he repeated. "You are mine to control, mine to play with, mine to use." With his free hand, he brushed the stray hairs from her face.

"I can't believe you have this...this...thing...in your house."

Some fear remained in her eyes but Rand also saw full arousal as her predicament registered just how open and vulnerable he had made her. Keeping her head in his hand for the moment, he slid his other along her belly to her exposed pussy. "Seems to me you like this...thing," he said softly as his finger dipped into her slit and found the wetness he knew would be waiting.

He didn't give her a chance to respond as he fisted his hand in her hair and rubbed her clit hard, watching how her face creased as her body reacted. Mercilessly pinching and stroking that hard little nub, he forced her close to an orgasm, listening to how her voice changed in the throes of pleasure, enjoying how her cries shortened as they increased in frequency and volume. Her head tried to move from side to side but his tight grip on her hair denied her even that movement.

Her eyes flew open and her breath caught as she balanced on the edge of coming and Rand looked into those unfocused eyes, enjoying the cruelty he inflicted on her by removing his hand from her clit. Her eyes sought his as her anguished cry filled the room and he smiled at her.

"Mine to control, to play with, to use."

He dropped her head back and straightened, walking away and out of her sight again.

"You bastard."

Rand grinned. "I'm glad you finally understand that."

The muscles of her arms were shaking and he lowered her body so that her back rested against the floor. He kept her legs and arms raised still—he wasn't through with her in this position yet. But letting her rest her weight and her head would allow him to proceed with his nefarious plans for the rest of her body.

This was so much more than Meg had expected, far more than she'd ever even dreamed, and she wouldn't trade one moment of it. From the unexpected roughness of his touch to the damn switchblade and now this machine that turned her into his puppet? Every moment focused her mind, bending it to his will. Even when forcing her body toward a climax he then denied, Rand Arthur dominated her far more than anyone she'd ever experienced in the past.

Music drifted through the room again—a slow, sensuous instrumental. The music faded to the background, however, when Rand stood over her, a large white candle in his hand. He bent down, smoothed the hair from her face with his free hand and checked her fingers. They'd gone numb as the blood drained out of them but even in her state, she knew they'd still be warm. For better or worse, she had time before getting the blood back into them became a necessity.

Rand leaned forward to capture her eyes with his before speaking.

"You are going deeper into subspace, slave. Gather your tensions — all the troubles at work, all the problems with family and friends. Gather all those thoughts into a nice little ball. Find every stray tendril of thought, tuck it neatly inside and then give that ball a nice, smooth surface."

Meg knew what he was doing. Using visual imagery to relieve stress was an old technique. But doing something so traditional at someone else's command, while chained and no longer in control of her body, made this particular use of the old trick unique. She closed her eyes, envisioned a blue ball about the size of a beach ball for all her stresses and pushed every stray thought inside. Her job, her mother, her parents' divorce, everything went inside the blue ball.

"Now shrink the ball, compact all those thoughts. Press out all the air between them."

Meg let out the air she hadn't even realized she'd been holding. Keeping her thoughts focused, she released her breath as she pressed the air out, not stopping 'til her lungs were empty and her stresses no bigger than the size of a softball.

"There's a timer on the ball. It's counting down. You see the explosives on the side of it. But you don't fear the explosion, you welcome it."

A small silver clock appeared in her mind, firmly attached to the side of the stress ball. She imagined the numbers flashing zeroes as she waited for his directions.

"There are five seconds left on the clock."

Meg changed the zeros in her mind's timer to five.

"In a moment, the timer will begin to count down. And when it reaches zero, the ball will explode and all the energy will course out through your fingers and toes. Don't fight it. Give the energy the channels it will need to leave your body."

Only Rand's voice touched her. Letting go another deep breath as her muscles relaxed even further, she opened her body and mind to the explosion to come.

"Five...four..." Rand's voice counted down the moments. Not seconds. More time elapsed than that between the numbers. But that was a stray thought and Meg pushed it into the ball along with the others.

"Three...two..." She hovered, waiting, her muscles relaxed and ready for the release to come.

"One...zero." Rand's fingers pressed on her clit and the ball exploded. Some strands of her orgasm sped along her legs and rocketed out her toes, some headed upward and out her outstretched fingers. A few looked for an easier way and shot out her mouth in a strangled cry. She relaxed her voice and the cry became a full-throated moan of release.

Her body caved in on itself only to expand again with a second blast of released tension when he rubbed her clit hard. The energy made arrows of her fingers and in her mind she imagined blue bolts shooting from them. Had anyone stood in her way, the darts of tension would have left them pierced and bleeding.

And just as suddenly, the energy ran out—a small fizzle, a pop...and then nothing. For the space of a heartbeat, her body remained extended before flopping into a heap of boneless flesh and blood. Only the cuffs around her ankles and wrists held up her limbs or even those would have collapsed.

Her pussy opened, her mouth hung slack. Even the muscles of her ass were open. Her body became a void that needed filling.

A low chuckle came from beside her and Meg remembered Rand. She opened her eyes, blinked a few times to focus on his face and gave him a tired smile.

Rand had used the technique before but never with quite such violent results. You needed a vivid imagination for such a visualization tool and apparently Meg had one in spades. He nodded at her murmured thank you, knowing from experience the emptiness that she would feel. If not given something to fill her spirit, it would be far too easy for those released tensions to creep back in and take over her soul once again.

But she had earned several moments of pure nothingness. This state often took hours to achieve and Meg deserved to float awhile before he replaced stress tensions for more pleasurable sexual ones. He'd appreciated her appearance as he'd undressed her but now he took his time as she drifted, noting subtleties he'd skimmed before.

The long, dark hair lay tangled around her head. He'd have fun brushing that out later. Her fairly round face gave way to a wonderfully long neck that just begged for a black leather collar.

He'd observed earlier that her breasts were a good size for binding with enough heft in them to give him something to work with. Now, however, he saw the large areolas and the soft nipples and the way her breasts rose and fell with the quieting of her breathing.

Her legs were still spread wide and he examined her shaved pussy, growing more delighted with his new sub by the moment. A bare pussy was always more fun to lick and tease and Rand decided that tasting that smooth skin would definitely be on the menu for the night's activities.

A big sigh came from the depths of her being as her body settled even deeper and Rand knew he needed to fill her psyche with new sensations. Otherwise, he risked her falling asleep, giving the tensions an opportunity to sneak in while she wasn't looking. She'd awaken feeling refreshed, yes. But without something to take up the spaces, that refreshment wouldn't last long.

He still held the candle in his hand and now he tipped it just a little, letting a single drop of white wax land on her breast. Her eyes flew open and he could see the confusion in their dark brown depths. He tilted the candle again.

Sharp stabs pulled her from her reverie. No, not stabs— stings. Little stings on her breasts. Rand loomed next to her and she remembered where she was. She'd almost forgotten. He held a white candle and tipped the taper toward her, dropping a bead near her bellybutton, trickling up to her breasts, dribbling into her cleavage. Each droplet stung, her mind convinced her skin burned beneath the hot wax, even as it cooled and hardened.

Now he turned the candle sideways, pouring the wax like a torrent over her breasts, splashing onto the areola as he moved the candle slowly, inexorably from one breast to the other. "Ouch...be careful!" She couldn't help the words. They tumbled out of her still somewhat unfocused mind.

Rand didn't stop. "I gave you a safeword and a safe gesture. Use them if you want. Otherwise...no."

His voice sounded rough and uncaring. The brute! Why had she ever agreed to this? She squirmed on the floor, her arms and legs jingling the chains above. When a drop of wax nearly hit her nipple, she cried out, despite her intention not to give him the satisfaction.

"If it hurts now, it's your own fault for not holding still."

Just like a man to try to put the blame on the victim, she thought. Still, she stopped thrashing and bore the stings as best she could. She'd show him who was boss here!

Rand saw the defiance in her eyes and stifled a chuckle, glad to see her independence rise to the surface when all else was gone. Proved she wasn't a doormat. But he needed her to understand she held no power, that her attempts were feeble and counterproductive. He held the candle a little higher so the wax wouldn't be as hot when it hit and let a drop fall directly onto her sensitive nipple.

"Ow!" Meg's face scowled and she wouldn't meet his eyes. He let another land directly beside the first. She turned her face from him. Deciding this game had just about fulfilled its usefulness, he let two more drops fall onto the other nipple, listening to her small gasps of surprise. But she didn't pull away from him again.

He stood, blew out the candle and put it back on the shelf beside the controls for his puppet machine. Flipping a few levers, he lowered her arms and legs, then went back to where she lay on the cement floor.

The cold of the hard floor seeped into her back. And she couldn't feel her hands or feet. When Rand lowered them, she made no attempt to move, not even to touch her wax-covered breasts. Not that she could have anyway. Pins and needles danced in her hands almost immediately, followed quickly by the ones in her feet. Rand knelt beside her to unfasten the cuffs from her wrists and every time he jarred her fingers, new waves of prickles flew from her arms back up the same channels she'd used to get rid of the tension.

"You're doing that on purpose," she accused.

"Doing what?" He wore a look of confused innocence as he moved to her ankles.

"You're not fooling me with that innocent act. Everything you do is calculated for effect. I've already figured that out. You're being deliberately rough taking these off to cause me more pain." She rolled over to her left, getting her freed right hand under her. Ignoring the darting pins, she struggled to sit up.

"Of course I am. You'll get the feeling back quicker than if you just lie here like a lump." As if to prove his point, he held one foot up and flicked the bottom of it. Purely on instinct, she tried to pull her foot away. He held it fast, however, and she went nowhere.

"Mmm...I like that reaction." He flicked at the heel again and watched her foot twist in his grip as she attempted to escape. "Does the other one do the same thing?" He picked up her other heel and flicked his forefinger at the sole of her foot, leaving the cuff alone for the moment.

"Stop it...ow!" She'd finally gotten herself into a sitting position, albeit an uncomfortable one. Leaning on the hand that felt marginally more awake, she raised her still-cuffed wrist and shook it. The chain rattled overhead and swung around in small circles.

"You really think I'm going to stop just because you tell me to?" Rand paused in the act of removing her ankle cuff. He seemed genuinely perplexed.

Meg shook her head, knowing she was about to lose a level of pretense. "No, I don't. I have a safeword and you have to trust that if I really need to stop, I'll use it. But saying 'stop' like that? I know I do it just to see if you'll listen to me."

Rand nodded. "Do you realize by now that I won't?"

Meg smiled slowly, understanding he'd stripped another layer from her and loving the fact that he had. First her clothes, then her dignity, then her stresses. Now her defenses were falling one by one. "Yes, I finally figured that out."

"Good." He let the foot he held fall to the floor. It landed with a thud and Meg winced at the pains that shot up her leg. But she didn't say a word and swallowed the gasp.

"On your hands and knees. Get that blood flowing in the opposite direction."

Only her left hand still tingled as she complied, taking a moment to push stray wisps of hair back from her face before getting on all fours. Rand moved behind her and she turned her head to watch him.

The contraption he wheeled out from the corner bore a vague resemblance to a chair but only if one used a great deal of imagination to picture it. The "seat" consisted of a very small block of wood and two planks that extended outward in a V-shape. The narrow back spread the width of two hands and from it, another two planks extended that paralleled the V below. Straps hung from various points and Meg knew immediately just how vulnerable she was about to be.

Rand wheeled out his torture chair, ostensibly examining the wooden supports and leather straps before putting it to use but in reality keeping an eye on his sub. She'd already surprised him with her resiliency, accepting his challenges even while calling him on them. Although he bound her body, she still hadn't given him her mind to play with. That little voice inside her head that analyzed what he did and chose from a menu of reactions hadn't yet shut down. Only when he'd managed to break through all the walls would she truly be free of her troubles. Time. That's all it would take. Time.

Time and a whole lot of patient work on his part.

Moving to stand beside her, he held out his hand and pulled her to her feet. "I've stretched your body and covered some of it with wax. Now it's time to bind your body, restrict all movement so that all you have control over are your thoughts." He pulled her close, feeling her wax-covered tits press hard against his shirt. Wrapping his arms tightly around her, he felt her hands come up in a feeble attempt to either hold him or push him away. She could do neither and he knew it. His voice dropped to a murmur in her ear. "Your mind is all that will be free in that chair. And even that will slowly bend to my will."

She whimpered in his arms, just as he hoped she would. A slight faltering meant her knees had gone weak at the thoughts he implanted. He tightened his embrace, knowing his bear hug made it difficult for her to breathe, but he didn't relent until he got a second whimper.

Making sure she could stand, he guided her to the tiny seat. She sat demurely, her legs tight together, not volunteering to put them along the wide spread of the seat, though she had to know that would be where they would ultimately end up. Rand just gave her a reassuring smile, brushed stray bits of wax from his shirt and moved to the back of the chair, throwing the wide waist strap around her middle and cinching it tight before she could protest.

Meg gasped and when she did, he pulled the strap tighter, sliding the metal prongs into the leather to buckle it closed. Another belt went under her breasts, pulling her back tight to the chair. Making sure her back didn't arch, he fastened the belt around her ribs as more bits of wax flaked off to fall onto the floor.

An evil little smile played on his lips as he readied the next belt, higher up the chair back. This wide one went around her neck and would force her to look straight ahead. She wouldn't be blindfolded but she wouldn't be able to see what he did either. Keeping a finger's width of space between the leather and her skin, he fastened it, pleased to hear a small sound escape from the back of that very throat he now controlled.

One more strap to further reinforce the total lack of movement—this one around her forehead. Now she couldn't even look side-to-side. Her eyes darted around, trying to keep her mind informed but bit by bit, he took away all her options.

Her arms came next. He quickly strapped each arm down at the biceps, elbow and wrist on the upper planks. Only her fingers could waggle at him. Effectively immobile from the waist up, Rand stood back to survey his handiwork thus far.

"Comfortable?"

Meg swallowed with a little difficulty and he saw the muscles contract as she tried to move her head. The strap around her forehead, however, prevented that. "Not sure that would be the word I'd use," she finally managed, her voice wispy.

Rand chuckled. "Good. Me either." He bent down in front of her, running a hand over her very shapely legs. He saw her shiver and decided to milk this further. "You know where these legs are going, don't you."

"I think I figured it out." Still breathless, her voice managed to convey the dry humor that Rand appreciated, yet knew he needed to temporarily disengage if he wanted her mind. Gently raising her left leg, he straightened it and bent down to place a gentle kiss right behind the knee.

She melted, just as he had planned. Little groans came from her as he pressed his nose against that wonderfully erotic area, his lips nibbling in exactly the right spots. Just before she had enough, he set her leg on the plank, reaching around for the strap and fastening it down at both the upper thigh and above the knee. A third strap fastened at the ankle.

"You bastard."

Rand laughed outright. "That's twice you've called me that. And yes, my dear, that I am." As if to prove it, he picked up the other leg, feeling her weight shift as she no longer could prop herself up and simply ran his fingers over the back of her leg before stretching her wide and fastening her down. Now all she could move were her fingers and toes.

Taking a quick inventory, he made sure all the straps up above were still good after the weight shift. They were and he stepped back to take another critical look at his new sub.

"No, something is still missing. Ah! I know what it is!"

Meg suspected Rand had known all along what he planned to do. His "thoughtful moment" didn't fool her. When he came back with the roll of wide red tape, she knew she was right.

"Love your voice, my dear. Don't care to hear it for a while though. If you decide to use your safeword, you're going to have to do so with your fingers. Left hand balled, thumb and forefinger out."

She couldn't move her head away and he slapped a strip of the tape over her mouth before she could say a word of protest. Two more strips, one above and one below, meant all she could manage would be a groan.

Meg tried to talk, tried to open her mouth. But the tape held fast and all she managed were some muffled sounds that meant nothing.

In fact, she meant nothing, she suddenly realized as she looked at him standing there, impassive. Her thoughts on how this thing should go, on the best techniques to remove her stress, were totally not wanted or needed. Rand had his own plans for her. In spite of herself, she felt her pussy cream.

"Those tits need to be cleaned. Too much wax still on them."

She watched him turn on his heel and move out of her line of vision for a few seconds. When he returned, he held a many-thonged flogger in his hand. A cry of protest sprang unbidden to her lips but, of course, came out only as a soft groan.

The first strokes, however, didn't sting as Rand trained his arm for the distance and force needed to remove the wax. She took some comfort from the total concentration on his face as he bent his thoughts on the task at hand, then realized that was exactly what this time together was for him...a task to be accomplished. When he finished Domming her, he'd tick their time together off his day planner as he would any other item on his to-do list. For a moment, she stopped watching him, lost in her thoughts.

She should have known better. The flogger snapped across her breast, sending wax flying in several directions. She jumped but savored the sting left behind as Rand again took several practice swings. And this time she saw the change in his eyes that signaled a stronger snap of the wrist.

Not that it made much difference. She still jumped, closing her eyes as the wax flew off and the stinging sank into her psyche. Apparently confident of his swing now, Rand slapped both sides of her right breast without pause. The remaining pieces of wax winged their way through the air like so many little butterflies and the pain built up until she couldn't stand it anymore. Her cry might be muffled, yet her anguish came out loud and clear.

To his credit, Rand's expression didn't change. He simply moved to the other breast, again taking his practice shots. Somehow knowing what was going to happen was worse, Meg realized. The flogger's sting was going to hurt and she had no way to prevent him from doing it. Even as the first harder blow fell, a white heat ignited between her legs.

Instinctually, she tried to arch her back, to move, to pull away from the onslaught, but the straps held tight and gave not even a quarter of an inch. She had no choice. Meg worked to let go, relaxing her body into acceptance rather than fighting the pain. As each blow fell, she let the harsh stings wash over her, channeling them to arrow straight to her exposed pussy, not even hearing her moans change tone.

Rand, however, was very aware of that fact. After an attempt at a squirm, she'd suddenly relaxed and the tenor of her sounds moved to a deeper range, signaling another layer of her defenses had fallen. Although only a few stray bits of wax remained scattered over her breasts, he continued to whip them, softly and often, with an occasional hard slap either right or left. The recently purchased deerskin flogger certainly lived up to his expectations. Keeping no meter to his strokes, his mind slipped into that magnificent state where he and the flogger became one.

Almost of its own volition, the flogger chose a different target. Moving to stand between her spread legs, Rand softly swung the flogger so the wide leather thongs swayed forward and back. He let the ends reach her pussy, tickle those lips and then descend, arcing back only to come up again with a little more force.

Her cry changed again. Deeper, more drawn out. The tips of the flogger colored as he continually tapped her waiting pussy. Briefly he thought of the clerk who had so eagerly volunteered his own back for Rand to use as a testing ground, sure that the kid would be disappointed to discover Rand used the instrument on a woman's pussy rather than a man's cock.

He listened to her breath catch, then turn to a sob as his torment continued. The beautiful lips between her legs were far too sensitive for beating but firm slaps that reinforced her helplessness served to heighten her arousal to the point of no return. They turned a healthy shade of pink, swelling as if to meet the thongs he wielded with such skill.

Her cries rose in pitch and frequency and Rand knew her climax hovered near. He increased the tempo, yet not the force, keeping time with her fevered noises. And when her muscles contracted in their bindings, he knew he'd pulled from her exactly what he wanted.

Meg panted for breath, her body and mind slowly recovering. Rand's methods might be crude yet Meg knew right then that she'd be back. Such an incredible ride deserved good service in return. As she came back to earth, she expected he would unbind her now, take his own pleasure and they'd be done.

But once again, he surprised her. She opened her eyes, wanting to thank him even though she couldn't speak the words. But he'd disappeared behind her and she couldn't turn her head to find him. In spite of the fact that she'd just come, her pussy spasmed again and moving on instinct, she tried to close her legs. But of course she couldn't and her body protested the fact while still being aroused by it.

His voice whispered softly in her ear. "I'm not yet done with you, slave. You are bound to my chair, bound by my hand. Your body responds only to my will."

The truth of his words sank into her soul. The whimper that sprang unbidden to the back of her throat voiced itself softly.

"You no longer even have a name, slave. You exist only as I make you exist. All you have, comes from me."

Her heart fluttered with a twinge of fear. What did he mean? What was he doing? Even as a small part of her rebelled, a larger part of her eagerly accepted his possession of her.

A black blindfold appeared in front of her. She wanted to scream, to tell him she wanted to keep that sense, since he denied her movement and speech. But choice no longer belonged to her. As the darkness descended, she knew she could use her safe gesture if she really wanted him to stop. Instead she balled her fingers into her fists and relinquished her sight to him.

He released her forehead belt so he could tie the blindfold on and Meg let her head hang forward a little. Not too far, the belt around her throat cut off her air if she moved too far. It was enough, however, to stretch the muscles of her neck a bit.

Such relief was short-lived, however, as he once again wrapped the strap around her head and belted her tightly against the chair once more.

Usually she could see a little light from the bottom of any blindfold, sometimes even see shapes through the mask Jack had liked to use. Rand's blindfold gave her nothing but blackness. She closed her eyes behind the blindfold and gave up trying to see.

A warm breeze blew across her pussy and she jumped. Not that she went very far but her body reacted anyway.

"Your lips are nicely swollen from my flogging, slave. Tender and ripe."

His voice came from below, from between her legs. Another breath blew across them and she started her climb once again.

"Mmm, your scent is very musky. Does your taste match your wonderful aroma?"

His tongue caressed her labia and Meg shivered, her body giving him more to taste as he pushed her arousal.

"Very nice," she heard him murmur. "Like a rare spice one finds only in a faraway, exotic land." His tongue dug deeper, scooping between her folds, and she moaned, giving him anew her soul to command.

Meg wanted to beg him to go faster but with the tape across her lips, all she could do to urge him on was whimper and moan. Her muscles ached but she didn't complain, her mind completely focused on his mouth and what he did between her legs.

His teeth now played with her pussy lips, biting down and pulling them to make her continually drip. She wanted him to stop playing and fuck her.

And then his teeth found her clit and enclosed it, a gentle bite that made her breath come in short gasps as she balanced on the edge. His tongue flicked against that sensitive bud in a barrage to her senses. In her bindings, her muscles bunched and fought as his tongue carried her desire higher. Mentally throwing her arms wide as she hovered on the brink, she reveled in the moment before leaning into the open space that gaped before her. And as she fell, sparks of relief radiated from his mouth on her clit to the tips of her fingers and toes, her body coursing with pleasure.

As she started to come down, he changed his tactic, plunging his fingers into her tight, wet pussy, taking his mouth away to rub his thumb over her clit and send her over a second cliff. He pushed relentlessly, forcing her to come again and again. She cried out, her voice reflecting her delicious agony. Four times, five—she lost count how many times she rose and fell.

Her cries diminished, her energy depleting rapidly with each orgasm. Even so, she didn't want them to end. The time between each one lengthened and Meg found herself grateful for the bindings that held her body upright.

Rand watched her come, trying to keep track of the total number of orgasms he gave her. He lost count after nine. My God, he'd never known a woman who could lose herself so completely in his hands! He found himself impressed more with her than with his ability to make her come.

The fingers of his hand puckered in her juices, like hands too long in water, as the seconds between each orgasm lengthened. Deciding he'd milked the last one out of her, he stood, crossed to a small table and used the towel covering some of his toys to wipe his hands before moving to the console and turning the lights down to a soft glow. His eyes never left her, however. The sheen on her skin that he'd admired before gleamed softly in the dim light. Her breathing became less labored but her muscles still twitched in their bindings in remembered pleasure.

Kneeling between her legs again, Rand began the process of releasing her from the chair. First her arms, placing them gently on her spread legs. Then her neck and upper body, though he did not remove the blindfold or the bondage tape across her mouth. She leaned forward on the tiny scrap of a seat and he waited to make sure she wasn't going to fall. When he'd removed the last belt, Rand took her hands in his. "Stand for me, slave."

He could tell she gathered her will for this simple task and when she stood, she teetered, off balance. He caught her to him and lifted her easily in his arms. Was it just natural for her to wrap her arms around his neck and snuggle into him? Or was something deeper going on? Rand had intended to make her dependent on him during their session and apparently, he'd succeeded.

But rather than the power rush he usually got at this point, something else tugged at him. A small lock of hair draped across her nose and he blew it gently since his hands were full. She turned her face toward him, pressing her cheek into his shoulder. That strange warm feeling hit him in the gut again.

He carried her over to the plush rug and pillows scattered in the corner. Laying her down, he caressed her eyes through the blindfold, her cheeks, her neck, her breasts, all the while talking in a quiet tone to her. He knew she barely heard the words, they weren't important. But the timbre of his voice, the softness of his touch — those spoke to her raw senses.

"I have you, you're safe. I'll take care of you, just listen to my voice. I'm here."

Gently he pushed off the blindfold, watching her blink in the dim light. "I give you back sight, slave, so you can see what you have become." He gazed down into her deep brown eyes, noticing the golden flecks that rimmed them, then looked deeper and saw into her soul.

A woman of passion rested there, a woman who too often put her own needs behind those of others. He had seen the restlessness in her before, now he saw what she could be when at peace with herself. Gently he removed the bondage tape from her mouth.

Her first words surprised him. "May I have a drink of water, Sir?"

Rand smiled. "You may, slave. Rest here and let me get it for you."

He laid her back on the cushions and unfolded a blanket to cover her before going to a small fridge he kept down here for snacks between sessions. Several water bottles, a couple apples, some grapes and cheese sat on the shelves. He picked up two bottles of water and returned to where she now lay calmly watching him. She no longer shivered as she started the long climb back to reality.

He gathered her into his arms, the softness of her hair brushing his cheek, then handed her the water she'd requested. She chuckled softly as she tried to open the bottle, then handed it back to him. "My muscles are like jelly. Would you please?"

Rand smiled and opened the bottle for her, holding it as she put her face up like a calf accepting milk from a bottle. He tipped a little water into her mouth, waited for her to swallow it, then tipped more in when she opened again. She shook her head after the second time and Rand recapped the bottle and set it beside him, opening his own and taking a long pull before once more cuddling his new submissive in his arms.

Meg snuggled in, her body nearly sated with all the times she'd come. Although she'd always been multi-orgasmic, today Rand had pushed the limits on that one. Never had she been so helpless before a man...and never had the man taken such full advantage. Smiling and letting out a big sigh, she rubbed her cheek against his shirt.

Shirt? Meg frowned and pulled back a little. "You're still wearing clothes?"

Rand looked down at her, his dark eyes amused. "Why wouldn't I be?"

"Well, because..." Meg faltered. Why shouldn't he still be in clothes? All Rand's attention had been on her and her orgasm. "Well, it's just that...I would think that..."

Rand pulled her closer. "Don't worry, slave. You haven't finished your duties yet." His hand stroked her hair. "Take this time to rest, to gather your energy. You will serve me soon."

Meg closed her eyes and sighed softly. His cologne smelled of power and money and for a moment, she indulged in a brief fantasy of herself as more than just a bottom to him. He called her slave but she knew that was only for effect and for the time they spent in a session. Rand was a Top to her, maybe as far as a Dom, nothing more. Soon their session would finish, she would go home and they wouldn't see each other again until the stresses built up one more time and she needed relief.

"I look forward to serving you," she murmured, almost wanting to get it over with as she reminded herself that this session had no importance except as a way to blow off steam. She wanted no commitments in life and neither did he.

"I like my serving girls bound and helpless. Are you ready to go back into bondage?"

Meg smiled at his silly question. "I am always ready to go back into bondage, my dear Sir."

He patted her rear and gestured for her to get up. "All right then, slave. On your feet."

Meg stood and watched as Rand pulled a harness down from the pegboard. She'd seen enough pictures that she recognized the armbinder at once. Some styles buckled the arms into place. This one, made of soft leather dyed a deep burgundy, laced like a corset for her arms.

"Turn around."

She complied without hesitation, putting her hands behind her back, palm to palm. He slid the leather glove over her arms and pulled the strings taut to encase her hands and arms in the binder. When he was done, he buckled a separate but matching belt around her waist, giving it a comfortable cinch rather than a tight one this time. He then brought a strap from the fingertips of the binder down through her legs and fastened it to the belt in front. She could barely raise her arms like this. The strap between her legs rubbed against her pussy and clit and Meg realized it might be possible to come if she could maneuver the strap just right.

No time to think of that now, however, as Rand gestured for her to kneel on one of the cushions. She did so and watched as he peeled off his shirt, revealing the muscles she'd felt but not yet seen. Strong shoulders tapered to a trim waist, a thin line of dark hair directing her sightline straight down.

He turned as he removed his pants and she wasn't surprised to discover he wore no underwear. If she were a Dom, she'd want to be ready to take the sub at a whim, so it made sense. With his back to her, she could admire the way his body moved, the strength she saw in the muscles of his back and the tightness of his ass. He had runner's legs, she realized, the upper thighs used to doing the bulk of the work. Rand's body was also lightly tanned from the sun—all over. No lines showed on his legs or on his hips to delineate the markings of a bathing suit and Meg realized that, on an estate this size, he must go swimming in the nude. The thought made her smile. But then he turned around and her attention diverted to his cock, rising as he stood before her.

The smile on her lips turned to a come-hither look as she watched his cock bloom with color, the veins turning into dark ridges that pulsed with power, the tip turning a deep burgundy to match her armbinder. He'd tasted her, now she waited, eager to return the favor.

Her hair still hung loose and she shook her head to get it out of the way. When Rand stepped closer, she licked her lips and opened her mouth, her eyes focused on the magnificent cock in front of her. He put his hand on the top of her head, using his other to guide his cock to her lips.

"Don't take it in yet. Lick me first."

She thought of the ice cream cones they'd eaten the first night they'd met and her tongue snaked out just as she had licked that colder treat. She swirled her tongue around the tip, closing her eyes and enjoying his clean taste. Definitely not a vanilla cone though. Licking down along the shaft, she found nuances of flavor, each one related and yet unique. The muskier, darker underside contrasted with the top where she savored the lighter taste that lingered in his skin.

But the tip remained her favorite and she returned there, her tongue finding the pre-cum that had formed in the slit as a reward for her efforts. Her lips closed over that velvety-soft skin as her tongue scooped out the present he gave her. When his fingers balled her hair into his fist, she knew she had scored.

His other hand now came up to the side of her head, also taking a fistful of hair to use as a handy guide for her head. Her pussy flooded at his rougher treatment of her and she moved the armbinder a bit, rubbing the strap against her clit.

Slowly, he moved her head back and forth, her lips rubbing over the ridge of skin at the base of the tip. Meg flicked her tongue against that sensitive round, loving the way his cock filled her mouth when he pushed in. But then he pushed deeper, that beautiful tip now showing the steel under the soft skin as he pressed his cock down her throat.

For a second, Meg was afraid she'd gag. Struggling against his hands, she took a deep breath in through her nose and forced her muscles to relax and accept him. And when she succeeded, he pushed past that reflex to fully possess her mouth.

She loved the length of his cock—probably seven or eight inches—as he managed to slide it all deep into her throat. She opened wide for him, impaled and unable to breathe with her nose buried in his groin. Above her, he grunted and pulled back, giving her only a second or two to grab a new breath before he buried himself down her throat again.

Meg's head reeled from the lack of air, her body protesting. Each movement made the belt slide over her now very lubricated pussy. Rand took pity on her, pulling in and out of her face in regular thrusts now, the sensitive ridge of skin rubbing against the entrance to her throat. She lost control of her movements, his hands in her hair her only guidance, her only way of staying upright.

Hot liquid filled her mouth, cascading down her throat. Instinctively, she swallowed, barely tasting the gift he gave her. Her body moved of its own volition, her arms sawing the strap over her clit until Meg enjoyed her own small climax as the evidence of Rand's orgasm gushed down her throat in waves.

She couldn't take all he gave her, however, and Rand pulled back, filling her mouth and watching the creamy white fluid leak out the sides. Her lips dripped with his cum and she ran her tongue over them to gather as much as she could.

Rand absently rubbed his cock as he came down from the height he'd climbed. His cum had splattered all over her cheeks and he grinned to see her flicking her tongue out to clean as much as she could reach. Letting go of her head, he threw his own back and let go an explosive sigh, closing his eyes and glorying in the exhaustive relaxation that filled the spaces in his soul.

Warmth encircled his cock and he looked down to see that Meg hadn't finished. She had inched forward and now her tongue caressed him again as she cleaned him, greedily taking in every drop that still clung to him. Resting a palm on the top of her head, he waited for her to finish, surprised anew by this gift of a woman. Mentally, he picked out the champagne he'd send to Jack along with a note expressing his condolences on the loss of a fine sub. Rand had no intention of giving Meg back when Jack eventually returned but he would be sure to compensate his friend while stealing his submissive.

Meg shivered again in her bindings so Rand took her shoulders and helped her to stand. He saw her wince as the strap between her legs pinched what had to be very sensitive lips down there. Unbuckling the strap from the belt around her waist, he slowly and carefully removed it, noting how she'd stained the leather with her juices. Chuckling, he began on the armbinder laces.

"I see it takes a lot to sate you."

Meg nodded, her heart rate returning to normal. "I'm afraid so. Haven't ever been fully...done...in my entire life. Give me five minutes' rest and I'm raring to go again."

Rand grinned. "I hereby take that as a challenge." He slid the leather off her arms and set the armbinder aside, coming back to help her massage her arms. Satisfied that her muscles were recovering, he led her again to the soft rug and the pillows. Throwing the blanket over the two of them, he spooned her into his arms.

"In fact," he whispered into her ear, "I'm not opposed to bringing in reinforcements in order to make sure you're sated."

She turned her face up toward him, her eyes already a bit dreamy with sleep. "Reinforcements?"

"Other men. Many men. Perhaps I shall arrange it…and you will service several instead of just one."

"Oh." Her voice came out breathless, almost as a whimper. Rand smiled and held her closer.

"I think you could take more than one man at a time, don't you?"

Meg nodded, her heart suddenly racing and her stomach doing flips in her belly. She'd fantasized about being the object of a gang bang before but to actually do it? Did she have the courage?

Meg yawned in spite of the new thoughts spinning in her head. She snuggled closer, feeling his cock nestle its way between her legs as she fell into the most relaxed sleep she'd had in a year.

Chapter Four

ဢ

"Yes, Mom, I'm coming up to see you this weekend. I promise. I'll leave tomorrow right after work and drive up."

"For the entire weekend? Oh Meg! That will be wonderful!"

Meg grinned at the obvious pleasure in her mother's voice and stretched her sore muscles as she undressed. Her workday had flown by with few problems and Meg felt as if she could do anything, tackle any problem. And dealing with her mother came first on the list. All thanks to Rand and his magic touch.

"See you Friday night then."

She hung up the phone and surveyed her guest room. A lonely spanking horse sat in the middle, currently draped with a few pieces of drying laundry. Off to the side, several coils of rope lined up on a small table testified to her undying desires to be tied up. The times she had spent here with Jack now seemed so…naïve. Rand had made her realize how much more existed out there for her. With a pang of regret, Meg realized she'd outgrown her mentor and now stood ready to accept challenges of a more extreme nature.

The phone in her hand rang and Meg almost dropped it in surprise. She checked the number and answered quickly.

"Evening, Rand."

He chuckled. "I called to see how you were doing. It's been a whole day."

"I'm still flying. Even just told my mother I want to visit for the weekend. She and I have some issues and I feel like I'm ready to tackle them."

"Great! Just remember, the euphoria you're feeling will wear off in a few days."

Meg grinned. "Well, then I'll just have to schedule another session, won't I?"

"Guess you will. Wondered if you were available for dinner tonight?"

"I am." She tried to keep the surprise out of her voice. While it was true she hadn't been able to keep Rand out of her thoughts all day, going out on a date with him hadn't really entered her mind. Mostly she just kept reliving the power in his arm and the roughness in his voice as he commanded her body and mind. But since he'd asked, she certainly wouldn't mind getting to know him on a different level.

"I'll be by to pick you up in half an hour then."

So soon? She hid her surprise, tossing off a casual, "See you then," before shutting the phone and racing to her closet.

It's amazing how many outfits a woman can go through in fifteen minutes. Meg pulled out and discarded three possibilities almost immediately. Too businesslike. The next two outfits actually got onto her body before being thrown onto a growing heap on the bed as too casual. Why hadn't she asked where they were going? Now she needed to find something that struck exactly the right balance between casual, dressed-up and I'm-ready-to-fuck-you-again-so-just-say-the-word.

Finally she settled on a gathered flowered skirt that hung to her ankles and a camisole top of a rich scarlet to match. A see-through blouse covered her shoulders but still allowed a good view of her cleavage. Satisfied that her look said "carefree and ready for fun", she went to work on her hair.

But she'd used up most of her time and she had little patience left. Pulling her locks into a ponytail and dashing on rudimentary makeup, she stood before her mirror to take an appraising look as the doorbell rang.

Rand looked marvelous in a light blue striped shirt, a dark silk tie, tied just loose enough to be casual, a look furthered by his turned-up sleeves. Meg got the impression he'd just thrown something on, unlike her own deliberations. But then he smiled and she grinned at her own silliness. How had she not noticed before how his eyes crinkled a little when he smiled? Or missed that little dimple that shadowed only the right cheek? Somehow the lack of symmetry gave him a rakish air and Meg remembered anew that he could be a very dangerous man.

"Ready?" He held out his hand and Meg nodded, putting her hand in his. Although only a few inches taller, somehow he managed to make her feel petite. She locked the door and they were off.

Rand studied the woman across from him as she pulled apart a crab leg to get at the meat inside. Jack was right. The woman bloomed in the afterglow of a good session. In fact, the dinner tonight had been Jack's suggestion when Rand e-mailed his thanks. A light had been turned on in her that he hadn't seen when they'd met for ice cream. Ice Cream Woman had been down-to-earth, sensible, almost pragmatic. The sexy creature who sat across the table from him now had lightened up considerably—just plain having fun and showing her sense of humor. Rand decided he'd like to see this woman far more often.

"Jack says hello, by the way," he told her.

Meg looked up in surprise. "He did?"

"He sent me an e-mail today. Said to say hello to you for him."

She frowned. "He could've e-mailed me too. He's only sent me one since he left."

"You sound upset by that." Rand didn't know what to make of her tone of voice.

"I am...a little. We're friends. I thought close friends. I've e-mailed him a couple of times but he's not writing back."

Rand cracked open another crab leg. "Well, if it's any consolation, he doesn't write much to me either." Silently he cursed himself for bringing up the subject of her former Dom. He knew they'd been together a long time. Could it be that the two of them had a stronger relationship than Jack admitted?

Meg shrugged but Rand could see she was still a little bothered. He put his food down and looked at her.

"Meg, if there's something between you two I should know about, I'd appreciate you getting it out now."

She shook her head. "He's my Dom and my friend. We're close. Or I thought we were. But no romance, if that's what you're afraid of."

"Not afraid. Just want to avoid problems down the road. And I'm sure he's just busy."

With a nod, Meg changed the subject and Rand understood she didn't want to talk about Jack right now. Deciding to leave the topic alone for the present, he went along, actually enjoying her knowledge of movies, both current releases and older classics. They talked about their favorite films and directors for the rest of the meal.

And when he took her home and they stood on her doorstep, he kissed her firmly, reminding her of the control he could exert when he wanted to, and took his leave before she could invite him inside. With her still reveling in the aftereffects of such an intense session, it would be very easy to take advantage of her. While tempted, Rand knew he'd pay in the end. So he contented himself with a sweet taste of her lips and left her wanting more. In other words, exactly as he felt.

* * * * *

The weekend with her mother had gone far better than Meg could have planned. It had taken several conversations to explain to her mother that she no longer wanted to hear her father referred to as "That Man" and that no one was against her if they spoke to him. In return, Meg had promised not to mention her father's existence to her mother. By the end of the weekend, her mother had finally conceded and when she needed to refer to her ex, had simply called him "your father". It was a huge step and Meg felt thrilled. She came home Sunday night elated.

No messages blinked on her machine but she did have an e-mail from Jack. Excited, she opened the note, only to feel a blossoming of disappointment at its shortness.

Meg,

Busy here. Polanski is great! A genius! Wish you could meet him. Make Rand treat you well for me. See ya!

Jack

She sighed, blowing the air out through pursed lips. Well, at least he hadn't forgotten her completely. Shutting down the program, she wrapped her good feelings around her, feeling discontent gnawing at the edges.

* * * * *

Monday morning dawned as a beautiful late spring day, not too hot, a gentle breeze swaying the trees. Meg inhaled deeply, ignored the dark earth of her garden calling her and forced herself into her car for the ride to her office, buried deep in the back rooms of Coughlin's main store. Of all the days to be stuck inside.

The traffic moved quickly, an advantage of going in to work just after rush hour. She'd gotten her muffler replaced last week and all was right with the world. Then why did she feel so uneasy? She pulled into the mall parking lot, found a space a distance from the store and turned off the car. Tension crept into her shoulders and she stared at the windowless building. With her new-found clarity, Meg finally faced up to the fact that she had grown to dislike her job immensely.

Not the customers, she loved working with people. Even the people under her were mostly fun to be with. No, the politics of the company got to her. The endless paperwork they forced her to do that smacked of old technology and outdated methods. And the daily grind of traveling from store to store, something she had enjoyed in the past, suddenly seemed wasteful of her time and energy.

Meg confronted a truth she'd been running from for months. She wasted her time here, having gone as far as the job could allow. For as long as she remained with this company, she would never do a different job, never face a new challenge. Just the same thing, over and over and over.

As she always did when this reality surfaced, Meg tried to shove it back down. "Stop it," she scolded herself. "At least you have a job. A good job. At a time when there are people with no jobs at all, you should be happy you have a paycheck."

But the words rang hollow today. Wasn't she entitled to…more? She was a hard worker and willing to pay the price. If she could only narrow her choices down to a single dream. Painter, sculptor, gardener—so many dreams, so little time to pursue them.

Meg shook her head. "Stop dreaming, woman. This is your reality. Deal with it." She got out of the car and slammed the door on them all. Setting her shoulders, she marched toward the store, a desperate determination in her step. Why did she feel as if she were heading to her doom?

* * * * *

Rand heard the change in her voice immediately. He'd called to see how the weekend had gone, wondering if her high had helped her with her mother. Apparently it had but something else had brought back the pragmatic side of Meg. Her sudden reappearance, and with such a vengeance, told Rand that something existed in his sub's life that she hadn't confided in him. Was she still upset about Jack not e-mailing her? He'd sent a quick note off to his friend giving him what-for about that topic. If he still hadn't e-mailed…

"Sorry, Rand. I'm just tired tonight, I guess."

"S'okay, Meg. I know a session can play havoc with a sub's emotional state and just wanted to check in on you."

"Thank you for that. I really do appreciate it. Did I tell you? Jack finally e-mailed me last night."

"Good!"

"All of three sentences but yeah. It was good."

Rand wanted to throttle his friend. Damn him! Jack knew better than Rand how emotionally fragile Meg might be, though she didn't strike Rand as the type who went to pieces when life got tough. To Meg's credit, she didn't waste time pouting about what life handed her. But tension colored her voice again and she definitely was putting him off. Rand decided to let it go. Whatever she was working through would probably come out in their next session. As long as he didn't wait too long to schedule it.

"Take the weekend off," he told her. "I'm going to pick up you up on Friday around seven and you're not going home until Sunday. Wear a mini-skirt and button-down blouse and nothing else."

"Rand Arthur, you cannot order me around like that!"

"Meg Turner, I just did."

He could almost hear her thinking in the silence that came from the phone. She gave a great sigh that told him whatever was going on was momentous for her. And when she acquiesced, he knew he would get her to confess all during their marathon weekend session.

"Friday at seven. Remember, only a blouse and skirt. Nothing else."

"I won't forget."

He flipped his phone shut and headed down to the dungeon. If he had his way, Meg was about to face the darkest parts of her psyche and in the process, experience one hell of a ride.

Chapter Five

ഇ

Meg threw herself into her work for the next few days, dealing with a late order, with reams of paperwork and with her increasing frustration, all while putting the finishing touches on the displays of new summer outfits that heralded the coming season. She stayed late and arrived early, wanting to have everything done so she could justify leaving early on Friday.

By three o'clock Friday, everything was as done as it was going to be and Meg flew out the door and hurried to her car. For once, the gods of traffic lights smiled on her and she made nearly every one of them on the way home. By the time she pulled into her driveway, her spirits had lifted.

Humming as she ran up the stairs, she had her blouse half unbuttoned before she paused just long enough to unlock the door and let herself in. Freedom! With each piece of clothing she took off, Meg found herself shedding more and more of her responsibilities until she stood stark naked in the middle of her bedroom. Throwing her arms out to her sides and grinning, she spun in a circle and fell backward on her bed, chuckling. Briefly she closed her eyes and breathed deeply as she thought of the freedom she'd have this weekend. No decisions to make, no customers to cajole or employees to deal with. Soon she'd be with Rand and give up all responsibilities in exchange for a few days of rest and relaxation.

This time she giggled in earnest as she sat up. Okay, so her idea of rest and relaxation didn't include the beach and a book or a bowl of popcorn and a movie. Hers involved whips and chains and all sorts of evil-looking torture devices. She looked over at the vibrator sitting on her nightstand and glanced at the clock behind it. She had plenty of time to give herself a good cum before she needed to be ready for Rand. But if she did, it might blunt the effect of anything he would guide her to tonight. Lightly fingering herself, she sighed and shook her head.

"Nope. Been good for three days, mostly 'cause I haven't been home. I can be good another three hours." Spinning on her heel, she headed for the shower.

When the doorbell rang, Meg answered, feeling a bit foolish. When Rand had given her orders to wear a mini-skirt, she hadn't wanted to admit she didn't own one. Several times during the week, she had gone over to a rack of short skirts in the store under the guise of deciding if they should be moved to a different spot. She'd rifled through them, giving them the casual once-over, as though trying to decide what should go on sale and what shouldn't. But in the end, she couldn't actually bring herself to purchase such a short scrap of skirt from her own place of employment. During her lunch hours, she had scouted the other department and specialty stores, finally finding a pleated plaid skirt that made her feel like she was back in her Catholic high school. A tight white blouse completed the schoolgirl/whore look.

Rand's appreciative examination was worth the effort, even if she couldn't stop blushing. He made her turn around in her doorway and then gestured her back inside. Stepping in, he set a small bag beside the door before following her through the arch that led to her living and dining rooms.

"Bend over, slave. Put your hands on the seat of that chair." He gestured to an extra dining room chair that sat against the wall between the two rooms.

Meg opened her mouth to protest, surprised they were starting this session so soon. Besides which, with this type of skirt you had to bend your knees down to pick something up, not bend over at the waist. Rand simply stood there as her mind adjusted to the sudden shift. Not entirely in sub mode, Meg's cheeks flamed as she stood before the straight-backed chair and bent over. The skirt rose up and gave Rand a clear view of her slit. With her legs tightly shut, however, she was certain he couldn't see more.

"Very nice. You did well."

She felt a small thrill of pleasure that her attire pleased him even as she blushed. Dressing like a slut wasn't easy for her. She had a position of responsibility and couldn't afford to lose it, no matter how much she disliked the job.

His hand slid under her skirt to caress her bare ass and Meg smiled. His firm touch knew just how to start the process that allowed her to relax.

"This is the state you should always be in, slave. Your body ready to serve at my command, your mind filled with nothing but the desire to please."

Meg nodded, letting the real world drift further from her thoughts.

His finger slid along her slit. "You're already wet? My, my."

Her cheeks flamed as she retorted, "Well, what did you expect? Dressed like this?"

He slapped her ass hard enough to leave a handprint.

"I expect my slave do what she's told and mind her tone."

Meg bit back another retort. He was right, of course. While not submissive in her real life, when sceneing, part of the fun came from giving up her innate feminism and letting him shoulder the burdens of existence for a while. Her tone had been snippy so she bore the mild reminder of her place without another word.

"Stand and turn."

His voice was devoid of the reprimand it had held a moment ago. She faced him, to find he didn't wear his Dom expression. In fact, he hadn't really been in full Dom mode since he'd walked in. Somewhat confused, she waited, her arms at her sides. When next he used her name rather than his normal term for her when they were playing, she understood that he postponed his Dom role to speak with her as an equal.

"Meg, I'm going to push your limits this weekend. It's Friday night and you're not coming back here until Sunday evening. You're going into tight bondage, into a world of sexual pain and ecstasy. I'm going to take you deep." He paused. "This will be a session like you've never experienced. But before we take one step more, you need to agree to it."

Meg considered. When he'd asked her to set aside her entire weekend, she hadn't really thought about the fact that he'd keep her in bondage the entire time. With Jack she'd never been in a session longer than twenty or so hours and that wasn't really continuous. Jack took lots of breaks and of course they slept for a good chunk of that time, resuming their play in the morning for another few hours. But what Rand had in mind was an entirely different beast altogether.

"Does my safeword still apply?"

Now it was Rand's turn to hesitate. Then he nodded. "Your safeword still applies."

From his reaction, Meg's heart quailed. The fact that he'd even considered pulling the safeword showed how serious he was. He intended to force her to face parts of herself she often ran away from and his pause showed his concern that she didn't have the courage to go there. Taking a deep breath, she let it out slowly, then raised her chin and looked him in the eye.

"Rand, thank you for the warning, I appreciate that. I won't say I'm not scared, because I am." She swallowed hard and continued. "I hereby give you permission to do whatever you want with me from this moment until Sunday, six o'clock in the evening."

The transformation as he once again allowed the Dom to come forth took her breath away. He grew even taller, his shoulders squared and his eyes turned to steel. "Then bend over again, slave. You need to finish dressing."

Mystified, she turned and again put her hands on the chair seat. She heard him rustling in the small bag by the door and when he slid a rubber dildo into her still-slick pussy, she shifted her weight and spread her legs a little to give him better access. By dropping her head, she could see what he did — the dildo connected to a length of leather and steel. He was going to belt that thing into her! Then a cold jelly hit her ass and he rubbed a second dildo along her slit. With a gentle push, he inserted the thinner dildo into her tiny hole and Meg stifled a gasp, wondering if she could really take all he had planned for the weekend.

"Stand."

She did, feeling the twin dildos move independently inside her body as Rand pulled the belt up between her legs.

"Hold up your skirt."

Rand fastened the chastity belt around her waist, making sure the leather fit snugly and wouldn't rub. He slid the tongue of the belt into the lock and she heard the snick that signaled her sex was now locked up tight. At his direction, she took a few experimental steps. While she wouldn't call the contraption comfortable, she also found it actually not that bad. The dildos' constant movement would make her pussy cream all night long and that was never a bad thing.

Rand adjusted her skirt to cover her ass once more and smiled for the first time since coming into her apartment. "You look beautiful."

Meg laughed at his comment and Rand loved the deep-throated sound. He watched her eyes twinkle as she pulled the skirt a little lower on her hips so that the fabric scrap would cover a bit more of her incredibly sexy ass. The men would be drooling tonight and he wondered what her reaction would be when they got to the club. While he normally didn't hang out in bars, this particular nightclub had already served as a wonderful setting for several of his scenes with past subs. The bartender and waitresses knew him well and were willing to turn a blind eye to some of the more extreme activities that took place when Rand visited. He also knew several of the men who hung out there and he counted on their leers to make Meg very aware of her sex appeal.

"Shall we go?" He gestured to the door.

"We're going out in public? Dressed like this?" The incredulity made Meg's voice rise a full octave.

"What did you think we were going to do?"

He saw her glance down the hall as she stuttered an answer. "I thought...thought that..." Turning back to him, she set her jaw and smiled. "Never mind."

What had she been thinking? He wanted to know her secrets. Only that way could he craft a weekend that would allow her to face her demons. Rand gestured along the narrow passageway. "Show me."

Color came up in her cheeks again. He liked that blush of pink on her and when she stammered, "No, that's okay. Really. I mean, you don't have to..." he simply stood and enjoyed her sudden discomfiture.

"Show me." Rand deliberately kept his voice pitched low and neutral, shading it with just a touch of command. A good Dom knew that all battles weren't worth fighting. That was a trap many wannabes fell into. Insecure in their own authority, they would push their subs on every matter, every time. As a result, the sub either turned into a doormat who wouldn't move without being told or would hightail it away from the control freak. Rand had seen both happen far too often.

At the moment, however, Rand didn't know if this was an issue he needed to push. If she remained adamant, he decided he wouldn't fight her on it. Let her win this one so she could "lose" others. Giving her one more opportunity, he stepped closer, repeating the words softly. "Show me."

To his surprise, Meg capitulated. "Fine. But know it isn't much and I'm not topping from the bottom. I just thought you wanted me to dress like this because of some role play you wanted to do and that we'd play here." Turning on her spiked heel, Meg led the way down the hall to a closed door. Giving him a glance and a shake of her head, she threw the door open and stepped inside.

The pieces were rudimentary and a bit crude, definitely not the best quality but serviceable nonetheless. He saw her swipe something off the spanking horse and toss it into the corner and fought down the desire to laugh. Laughter certainly wouldn't be taken the right way at the moment. He didn't want her to mistake his mirth for making fun of her elementary dungeon.

"You and Jack used to play here?"

"Sometimes. More room here than at his loft, although we had to time our scenes for when no one was home downstairs."

"And is anyone down there tonight?" He cocked an eyebrow at her as if he were considering the possibility.

"No. They went to dinner and the movies. Won't be back 'til after midnight." She shook her head. "It's all right, Rand. We don't have to play here. What I saw of your own personal dungeon makes this pretty pitiful in comparison."

"We won't be playing here but not for that reason. For the record, I don't think it's pitiful in comparison. You've done what you could in the space open to you." His gesture took in the room. "So no judgments there. No, we won't be playing here for an entirely different reason."

"And what is that?"

"Very simply, because this is your turf. You're familiar with these toys, you know what each one is and what it can do to you and for you. In short, you're comfortable here."

"And you want to move me out of my comfort zone." Meg smiled at him, was that a look of relief on her face? He stepped to her and pulled her close, liking the way she fit into his arms.

"I want to move you far out of your comfort zone, Meg Turner."

She shivered, as he'd hoped. "And that means going out in public, dressed like this?"

"It does."

For a moment, Rand thought she might refuse. Although she didn't pull away, her eyes dropped, as did her chin and shoulders. Was she looking for courage? Or a reason to refuse him? Demanding patience of himself, he simply waited as she considered.

Finally, with a deep sigh and a shake, Meg straightened and looked him in the eye. "Then let's go."

Rand didn't say another word, only gestured to the front door. He watched as she tried desperately not to swing the skirt as she walked, the twin dildos locked inside her rubbing together no matter how she held herself as she moved, no matter how small a step she took. At his pickup, he held open the cab door, blatantly admiring the view as she gently hitched her rear end up onto the seat, being sure that she noticed him watching her paltry attempts at dignity. That, at least, got a laugh out of her.

"This is silly, I know. Lots of women wear short skirts."

"Yes, but lots of women wear some sort of underwear under them." Rand pushed the door shut and let the comment work on her imagination as he walked around the truck.

"Well, I have something like underwear on underneath," Meg retorted when he got in the driver's side. She shifted her position, leaning to one side and Rand knew she tried to adjust the dildos' position to her advantage.

"No coming unless I give permission," he warned.

"I figured that." In the streetlights, he saw her naughty smile. "I'll be good on that one, don't worry. Like the payoff too much to disobey that rule."

Rand backed out of her driveway, heading up Park to Monroe Avenue, home of the city's offbeat shops and aging hippie population. Tattoo parlors and piercing joints sat side by side with bookstores and bagel places, the occasional adult toy shop thrown in for good measure. When Rand turned toward downtown instead of out toward the suburbs, Meg looked at him in confusion.

"Where are we going?"

"Cloud 18."

Meg almost choked. Everyone knew Cloud 18 was the number one place to go in order to hook up with an easy lay for the night. She'd heard all sorts of rumors about the activities that went on inside but had never had the courage to actually go in. She certainly would never go into such a club by herself. Even when she did go out with some of the girls from work, she never even considered mentioning this place as a possible destination. The women who went there were sluts and the men free with their hands from all she'd heard. She balked.

"No. I am not going in there wearing this skimpy little skirt."

Rand didn't answer as he drove the last few blocks to the club. He pulled up to the curb as Meg stared at the building, the neon lights over the front door giving her face a ruddy glow. Leaving the engine running, he got out of the truck, handed his keys to the valet and came to open Meg's door. He held out his hand and waited. Meg bit her lip and hesitated, finally putting her hand in his and letting him help her out. She'd worn spike heels and now teetered a moment as she fought to keep her pleated skirt down in the sudden breeze.

"You wear a belt for a reason, slave. You are to let any man touch you in any way he wishes. The belt will keep them from going too far." He took her chin and tilted her face up to his, bussing her lips with a quick kiss. "Trust me."

"Trust him," she muttered as she followed him into the den of iniquity, her hand holding tightly to his as if it were her lifeline. "I'm dressed like a slut, he wants me to act like a slut and he says, 'trust me'." She shook her head. "I am out of my mind."

Stress Relief

He pulled her in front of him as the bouncer at the door ushered them past the waiting line and whispered in her ear. "You are out of your mind, slave. Your mind is mine. Remember that."

The first five minutes had been the worst, Meg decided. They had stood at the bar for that eternity, everyone in the place giving her the once-over before Rand led her on a meandering route through the tables to a booth in the back.

Men openly ogled her, sometimes starting at her toes and working their eyes up to stop at her breasts, sometimes starting at chest level and going down in a long, lingering gaze. Few of them actually looked at her face and Meg found herself a little put out at that. She could be a dog and as long as she had curves in all the right places, they wouldn't care. She went from being self-conscious about her skirt length and low-cut top to being ticked that they only appreciated her from the neck down.

Still, she felt grateful when they finally arrived at the secluded circular booth in the back. A hideous neon-green tablecloth covered what was sure to be a cheap table, its ends draping the floor to puddle in a circle. The booth itself, upholstered in fine burgundy leather, however, provided a decided contrast to the tablecloth. Rand slid in first, gesturing for Meg to join him on the edge. With the entire booth empty, she was tempted to make him move over and then remembered—she was here in submission. Tucking as much of the tiny skirt under her rump as she could, she took a demure seat.

In seconds, a handsome young stud wearing a tad too much bling stood by her side. He barely glanced at Rand, his eyes fixed on Meg's chest. "Wanna dance?"

She started to shake her head no but Rand pushed her toward the creep. "She'd love to."

Darting daggers at him, she turned back to the overly hip kid, standing when Rand pinched her ass. Biting back the yelp, she shouted over the music. "Let's go."

81

The erstwhile Romeo certainly had his timing right. Just as they arrived on the floor, the song ended, quickly replaced by a ballad. Grinning, the creep pulled her tight. Surprised, Meg discovered there were muscles under that silk shirt.

"Name's Tad. But you can call me anything you want."

Meg rolled her eyes. He held her so tightly to his chest that her chin rested on his shoulder. She sighed and decided to just bear it.

The song slipped into the second verse and so did Tad's hand, sliding down her back to cup her ass cheek. Automatically, her arm reached to move it back up, when she caught sight of Rand in the corner. He shook his head and she remembered she was to let men do what they wanted tonight. Tonight she was nothing more than a slut in a chastity belt.

Meg grinned. The idea did have certain merits. She could go all the way to third base and never have to worry about reaching home with any of them. She could tease and flirt all she wanted. She swayed her hips a little more provocatively.

"Oh yeah, baby. Nice moves."

Both hands now gripped her ass and Meg tucked her head toward Tad's. "I like a man who knows how to dance."

For answer, Tad ground his pelvis into hers and Meg felt his hard cock press against her belt. In spite of her decision to enjoy the flirting, she blushed with a little shame that she had caused that reaction, when there was no way she'd be finishing this. Tad, of course, misinterpreted the blush.

"Come home with me, baby, and I'll see you get that all night long."

She shook her head, feigning regret. "Sorry, but I'm with him." With her chin, she gestured to Rand, who sat watching their every move.

The song ended and Tad's fingers brushed against her breasts as he released her. Entwining his fingers in hers, he took her back to the table.

"She dances well, doesn't she?" Rand asked the young man.

"That she does, old man." To Meg's alarm, the kid put his arm around her shoulders and pulled her close. "She needs someone who knows how to treat a lady."

Rand laughed. "She's no lady, believe me. Come on, have a seat and I'll buy you whatever you're drinking."

Meg was appalled. Rand slid in, giving Tad room to sit. The creep slid in beside him, then had the audacity to pat the tiny scrap of leather they'd left for her to sit on. She'd more or less be in his lap. A stern look from Rand, however, and she shut her mouth. She'd given him permission to command her for the weekend when she thought they were going back to his place and play in that wonderful dungeon of his. This kind of play had not been on her mind at all. But now that Rand had introduced the idea…Meg decided to play the scene out a little farther and see where he wanted to go with it.

As Tad's hand slid under her skirt and cupped her bare ass, Meg gritted her teeth and reconsidered her decision. Rand told her she would face some of the darkest parts of herself and here she was, dressed as a tart and letting some guy feel her up. She ducked her head to hide a smile. There was no doubt the thought of being so incredibly naughty did turn her on. Suddenly feeling wicked, she leaned her elbows on the table and adjusted her position so that she sat directly on Tad's leg, her own spread wide. With any luck, her pussy juices should leave a nice big stain on the front of his khaki pants.

"Another beer for our friend," Rand called to the waitress, who brought a tall glass and a bottle over and set them on the table. The woman grinned at Meg and gave her a wink as she turned and headed back to the bar.

"Rand! Haven't seen you in here in a while!"

Meg gave the blond guy who approached the booth a once-over, taking note of the short hair, the clean chin, the twinkling ice blue eyes and the dimple in his chin. The suit was tailored, the tie, silk. She was pretty sure this one had muscles in all the right places too. Shifting again, she swung her leg around so that she sat more demurely beside Tad and smiled at the stranger as she waited to find out who he was and what he wanted.

"Hey, Sam, good to see you!"

The two shook hands and then Rand gestured to the booth, sliding over as he did so. "Join us!"

Tad moved over, Meg did too, and Sam slid in beside her, giving her body a more-than-casual glance. "I like the set dressing you're hanging with these days."

Meg opened her mouth to protest but before she could, Rand introduced Tad. As Sam leaned over to shake hands, his arm brushed her boobs as if by accident. Meg knew otherwise. She gritted her teeth and kept her mouth shut. Flaunting herself was one thing, having this guy assume he had certain rights because of the way she dressed was something else entirely.

"Pete joining you tonight?"

Rand nodded. "He's usually here on Friday nights."

"Tad, you're a newbie in Rand's circle. You're in for a good time."

Meg had no idea what this guy was talking about. Sandwiched between a creep and an arrogant jerk, Meg couldn't decide which was worse. When Sam's hand rested on her upper thigh and quickly moved up to find the chastity belt, Meg knew the answer.

"The man has talented fingers, slave. Let him explore."

Meg's head whipped around at the name he gave her. How dare he? In public, to these strangers! For several seconds their eyes held in a contest of wills, Meg's eyes flaring with anger and humiliation and Rand's holding a look of challenge.

In the end, it was that look that made her capitulate. If he'd been full of himself and lording it over her, she would've walked out the door and that would have been the end of any further contact. But he wasn't. He simply provided challenges and she could choose to accept them or not. Everything remained her call.

She broke eye contact to scan the crowd as she regained her composure. Tad didn't notice but she knew Sam watched her reactions. When she sighed and dropped her eyes to her hands, folded on the table, Sam's fingers probed the belt, sliding in between her skin and the leather.

Arousal shocked through her and her eyes went wide as his index finger found and pressed on her clit. Instinctively, her legs spread a bit wider in the tight spot she was sandwiched into. When Tad's eyes fell to her lap and he realized her skirt was pushed all the way up, he too turned toward her. She saw him look at Sam, who gave him an evil grin and nodded.

Now Tad's hand slid down and under to feel the wetness the two of them produced. Meg's nipples hardened and she knew they noticed the two hard nubs pushing out the fabric of her shirt.

"Too bad this place doesn't have a wet T-shirt contest," Tad whispered in her ear.

"I think we can take care of that." Before she realized what Sam meant, he had flung her arm over his shoulder and made a dive for her chest, fastening his lips on her nipple, pulling it into his mouth through the thin cotton fabric. Even as she whimpered in her excitement, Meg's hand came down to bat his head away.

But Tad learned quickly and he too pushed her arm out of his way, pinning it to the seat while grabbing her tit with his free hand and pulling it toward him. The warmth of his breath caressed the nipple a moment before sucking it hard into his mouth. But where Sam used only his lip, Tad bit down and she squealed before she could hide it.

Rand watched the two suckle Meg's covered breasts in public, her frantic eyes scanning the crowd to see if anyone noticed. He wasn't worried. The angle of the booth meant few could actually see what was going on. The management charged quite a bit of money for this particular table and Rand knew the location was worth every penny. Meg's eyes sought his and the look she shot in his direction bordered on panic, yet he could see her eyes were already a little unfocused as her body responded to their touch. He toasted her with his glass and watched as they forced her to come.

The loud music covered her quiet moans of pleasure as she melted under their pressure. Was there anything more beautiful than a woman in the throes of ecstasy? Her eyes closed and her head fell back as she stopped fighting them and let them carry her along. His own cock grew hard watching her being serviced by strangers and when she came, he decided she was ready to be pushed to the next level.

Two grinning heads pulled away from her breasts at nearly the same time, leaving two large wet spots on the front of her blouse. Her nipples stood in sharp relief and Rand knew they'd be reddened and sensitive after their recent use. Sam pulled his hand from her lap and presented his fingers to her lips and when Meg looked over at Rand, uncertain, he nodded, giving her permission. With a tentative tongue, she licked her juices off Sam's fingers.

Tad, of course, presented his hand to be cleaned as well. Rand smiled like a benevolent mentor teaching a pupil. Tad learned quickly and had certainly lived up to his hopes for him. People like Tad existed in every social class—toadies who just came along for a free ride or in this case, a free feel. Rand didn't mind. Toadies had their uses. Like Sam. Rand knew Sam from past visits to the club and knew he could count on the man to play along.

With impeccable timing, the waitress came over to replenish the drinks. With an inviting lift of her eyebrow and bounce of her hip, the woman let Rand know she was available if he needed another playmate. Rand gave her a generous tip and considered her an ace in his pocket.

"Yeah, you certainly do have some nice set dressing, Rand."

"Slave, you didn't say thank you to our guests."

He loved how she blushed when even mildly reprimanded in public. "Thank you both, very much," she murmured, her eyes downcast and her hands back on the green tabletop. Time to push her limit.

"I think they need a better thank you than that." He held up his hand when she started to repeat her words a little louder. "No, slave. Not like that. On your knees."

He saw Sam's face split into a wide grin. He knew what was coming. Rand had brought women to the club before for use. Usually at their insistence. Several women he knew had begged for public play and as long as the customers paid, this club not only allowed but encouraged it.

When Meg hesitated, Sam lifted the green cloth and Rand gestured to the open space. "Underneath."

He watched the war of emotions play over her features—shock, anger, arousal, anger, desire, shame, anger, need, acquiescence. With another glance in the direction of the general public, she slid down under the table, almost gratefully, and Rand understood. Under there, whatever was required of her would at least be shielded from view. She could pretend none of them were there. He grinned at the other two men, knowing they were both so hard they were ready to burst. He almost felt sympathetic for the woman who was on her knees under the table. Almost.

He lifted the cloth and bent down to give his instructions. "As you can see, these men are in need of some relief and you are to thank them properly. Use only your hands. Wear their present to you on your chest...and let none of it stain their pants. Take care of our guests, slave."

Chapter Six

ဢ

For several seconds Meg sat in shock. Was this really her? Had she just really come in front of a room full of people? Did he really expect her to give hand jobs to these two total strangers?

Strangers who, until a moment ago, had their fingers on her pussy. Her body spasmed in memory and Meg shook her head. Yes, he expected it, and yes, she was going to do it. Taking a deep breath and deciding Tad had the least control, she reached up and gingerly unzipped his pants.

Not surprised to discover the Romeo wannabe traveled commando, she crept as close as she could, mindful that Rand didn't want any of the men's cum to land anywhere but on her chest. She'd always suspected the size of a man's cock was inversely proportional to the size of his ego and Tad's cock proved her theory. While not tiny, he wasn't much more than a handful and Meg closed her fingers around him, trying not to make a face of disgust.

As she pumped, she tried to figure out who she was more disgusted at. Rand for commanding her to do this, herself for allowing it or Tad for...well, for just being there. She supposed, really, that he held the least blame. What man wouldn't sit for a hand job when freely offered? Pre-cum formed at the small slit and she rubbed her thumb over it, squeezing his cock a little harder.

His cum spurted out in fitful gobs that splattered on her already-wet blouse. Sticky and warm, the liquid ran down her cleavage, leaving wet white trails. When the last few spurts didn't have enough force to go far, Meg caught the cum in her hands, mindful to keep his trousers clean, although the drying spot on his leg from her pussy gave her a small feeling of triumph.

Tad leaned back and looked down at her, a silly grin on his face. In fact, all three of them watched her and she realized her seclusion under the table was really a sham. None of them made any pretense about what she was doing down there and even though the other patrons couldn't currently see her face, they would know what she'd done for sure when she crawled out, covered in cum.

She held up her sticky hands to Rand, intending to ask him for a napkin, but he gave her instructions before she could ask. "That's what you have a skirt for, slave."

Closing her eyes and gritting her teeth, Meg took a deep breath, opened her palms and hesitated, her hands over her hips. It wasn't the skirt. It hadn't been that expensive and the fact she was about to ruin it didn't matter. It was the feel of the sticky stuff on her hands. Ever since she was a kid and did finger painting, she'd hated anything gunky on her hands. Her mother had been furious at the unsatisfactory art grade she'd brought home from kindergarten because Meg had refused to put her hands in the paint. She knew Rand had no idea of her revulsion of thick liquids dirtying her hands but the fact remained that she hated what she was about to do.

Taking a deep breath, she slammed her palms onto her hips and slid them along the fabric to wipe off most of the now-cold cum. God, she hated this feel! Swallowing hard, she cleaned her hands.

"My turn."

She looked up to see that Sam had already undone his pants and pulled out his cock. This was a man to be reckoned with, his cock long and thick, the ridges standing out like little mountain ranges. Giving her hands a final swipe, Meg closed her eyes and steeled her nerves for a second time.

Sam was more experienced and took his time coming. So much so that Meg's arm began to ache. Yet she kept up the pressure, desperately wanting him to come. And when he did, it was no small amount like Tad had given her. Sam's cum seemed to spurt in buckets, wild and uncontrolled. A gob landed on her chin and Meg turned her head. But that made things worse as he kept coming and white liquid coated her hair. Tears sprang to her eyes as she tried to direct the cum and failed. By the time he finished, her blouse, her neck, her chin were all covered. It dripped from her chin to splash against her chest and run down her stomach. She reeked of men's use of her and she sat back on her heels, tears pouring down her cheeks, her cum-covered hands palm up on her soaked skirt.

Rand recognized at once that he'd pushed a little too far. Wetting a cloth napkin, he dropped it down to her. "Wash your hands, little one. You did well."

He waited until she'd cleaned her hands and wiped most of it from her chin and chest before he stood. "I trust you had a good time, gentlemen?"

Tad still wore the silly smile and Sam just sat with his arms spread out along the back of the booth. Both nodded.

"Give my best to Pete when he gets here and tell him he was too late," Rand told them as he threw a large tip on the table for the waitress. He bent down and pulled up the tablecloth, offering his hand to help Meg out from underneath. Still sniffling, she came up, looking bedraggled and well-used. Exactly where he wanted her to be.

The back exit from the club stood only a few feet away and Rand steered her toward it as the only concession he would allow her for her appearance, quickly walking up the alley to the front of the building where an entire line of hopefuls waited their turn to get in. She kept her back to them, trying to hide the mess. The warmth of the night meant she hadn't brought a jacket, an oversight she now regretted.

As if waiting for the valet to retrieve the truck wasn't bad enough, Rand took time to strike up a conversation with the other attendant. They exchanged pleasantries about the evening and Meg wanted to find a hole to crawl into, sure that everyone in line saw and snickered at her cum-covered appearance. The attendant's leer only added to her humiliation.

But when the valet pulled the pickup to the curb and Rand went to the back, opened the hatch and gestured for her to get in, Meg's humiliation was complete.

"You're not sitting in the front looking like that, slave. You'll ride home back here."

It was the totally dismissive tone of voice that got her. That and the smirks from the two valets. Her embarrassment turned to full-fledged anger and she stalked her way to the back of the truck. "Fine. I've had it with you. I wouldn't ride in the front if you begged me."

"I don't beg," Rand said, just for her ears. "You do."

"Not on your life!" she retorted, sitting her rear end on the metal tailgate. But the cold metal made her squeal and stand right back up, ruining her high dudgeon. The leering valet laughed outright. Glaring, Meg sat again. But then she realized that, no matter how she crawled into the dark interior, the hovering valets would get a clear view of either ass or pussy. She chose ass.

Flipping onto her knees, she crawled in and sat alone in the dark as Rand closed up the tailgate and hatch.

Left to her own thoughts, Meg took stock, her anger firing her up. She'd been called a slave in public, not once but several times. She'd danced with a creep whose wandering hands made her feel like a cheap slut. Instead of standing up for her, Rand had then invited the creep to join them, eventually commanding her to give two strangers hand jobs and to wear their cum on her chest.

The closed space reeked of their scent. Meg fumed as Rand started the truck. Pursing her lips, she fired off a one-finger salute to the two at the curb as they pulled away. Even if the tiny tinted windows meant they couldn't see her, it still felt good and Meg grabbed at every straw of dignity she could find.

What was Rand doing to her? And why was she letting him? "I'm going to take you deep," he'd told her. Well, she'd never been so humiliated in her life. She could have stopped the whole evening with a word. So why hadn't she?

Because on a deep level inside, she had enjoyed it. Meg bit her lip and watched the scenery go by backward as she admitted much of it had been pleasant. Certainly their fingers hadn't been awful. In spite of her anger, she grinned in the privacy of the truck bed. She'd definitely liked that part—such a totally naughty thing to do. And the concept of giving hand jobs to strangers made her pussy ache around the dildo she wore. If he ever commanded her to do such a thing again, Meg knew that not only would she do it but she'd enjoy the experience a whole lot more.

She leaned her back against the cab and tried to find a comfortable place to sit. The skin around her ass burned from the rubbing of the chastity belt and she needed to experiment with several positions before finding one that allowed her to stretch her legs and yet keep off her rear end. Lost in her thoughts, the turn into Rand's estate took her by surprise and she teetered over, catching herself before she face-planted on the floor of the truck bed.

Meg welcomed the fresh air that came in when Rand opened the back of the truck. With a single word and gesture, he made it clear that their relationship hadn't changed. "Out."

Not caring if she acted like a lady by this point, Meg crawled out of the truck, still unsure exactly how she felt concerning tonight's activities. But she followed his orders, curious to discover where this journey would take her. He'd already disturbed her deliberately calm demeanor several times tonight. With renewed determination, she stood in the driveway in front of his large garage and waited.

"This way." Rand stepped off quickly. As last time, he didn't look back, simply assumed she would follow. But he didn't lead her into the house, instead he headed around the garage to a patio in the back. Scattered lounges and chairs interspersed with small tables created a quiet, outdoor living space bordered by an in-ground swimming pool. She didn't get much of a chance to enjoy the view, however, before he again gave her a perfunctory command, "Strip."

She'd never been naked in the moonlight but didn't care in her rush to get rid of the offending clothes. The blouse stuck to her skin and she had to peel it off her breasts where the cum had hardened. Dropping the two pieces to the ground with a sneer of disgust, Meg shuddered and kicked off her shoes as well. The belt around her waist was locked on, so she didn't make any move to remove it.

"Time to clean you, slave."

Meg turned to the pool, grateful for a chance to skinny-dip and clean off what remained, so the blast of cold water that came out of the darkness and hit her body with enough force to push her back surprised the hell out of her. She squealed, turning away and trying to scamper away from the cold stream that insisted on following her, running up and down her body. Her fault for not paying attention to him while she undressed, she supposed. She ran to the side of the patio to escape the cold water but Rand stayed with her. In desperation, she took cover behind a padded chair in an effort to escape the frigid water, wondering why she hadn't dove into the warm pool as soon as the cold water hit her. Now he cut off her escape to that respite. When Rand brought the hose around the side of the chair, she ran to a tree on the edge of the patio.

As quickly as it started, the water stopped and Meg stood still, shivering in the dark, under a tree to the side where she had ultimately taken refuge. "Rand, that was totally uncalled for. Yes, I need a shower but from the garden hose?" She saw Rand drop the hose and pick up something small from the table on the patio before coming over to where she stood.

93

He didn't say a word. In the moonlight, she could see the power in his step as he strode across the space between them and Meg took a step backward. Before she could speak again, he'd grabbed her arm and flipped the handcuff onto it, dragging her back against the tree.

"What are you doing? Ouch!" The rough bark of the tree rubbed against her naked body and she fell off balance. Rand took the opportunity to get hold of her other arm and pull her back, locking her wrists together behind the tree.

"If you're not going to stand still willingly, then it will have to be against your will," Rand informed her as he came around to stand in front of her again. Meg now had her feet under her but he was afraid she'd scrape her back on the bark. He had simply intended to wash her with the hose and be done with it, handcuffing her to take her inside, except then she'd run away from him and he didn't want to chase her all over the estate. Could he now turn this to his advantage, use it to push her so much further?

He pulled the hose over as she kept up a continual protest. "Rand…look…this really isn't necessary. I can wash myself. The water's too cold to do a decent job anyway." When he didn't show any sign of listening, her tactics changed from using logic to playing on his emotions.

"Please don't turn that hose on me. It's cold. I'm already shivering. Please, Sir?" The change of title had no outward effect. Because she didn't use her safeword, Rand ignored her babblings as just that—words she had to get out of her system. In fact, that was what this entire weekend was all about, getting her to rid herself of the baggage she carried. She claimed she only engaged in BDSM activities as a way to relieve her stress. If that were the case and she needed another session so soon after the first, then one of two things was going on. Either she lied about the reason for participating and she actually did scenes because she thoroughly enjoyed them, which meant the stress-reliever excuse was just that—an excuse. Or secondly, she carried far too much baggage with her at all times and the activities no longer worked to get rid of it. Either way, he was going to get to the bottom of Meg Turner before he was done with her. And if that meant pushing her to the breaking point over and over, then he was fully prepared to push.

He turned the hose on full blast in a steady, hard stream, pointing past the tree before bringing it to the left and over her shoulders and upper chest. She made the most delightful squeals, closing her eyes and turning her head to keep the water away. She was right, of course, the cold water wouldn't get her as clean as a nice warm bath, but then again, the nice warm bath wouldn't strip away her layers. Nor would letting her take a swim in the pool. He trained the hose to run down her legs, knowing the strong pulse of water would awaken her skin.

And if the water could awaken the skin on her chest and arms, just think what it could do to her pussy. Too bad that belt was still on her. He turned off the hose and dropped it to the ground.

"You bastard."

"You always say that as if you just figured it out. But I'm sure you're not that stupid, slave. You already know what I am, so I have to assume you mean that as a title now." He unlocked the small metal lock at her navel and slipped the belt loose.

"Take it any way you want. It doesn't change the fact that you have a mean streak in you."

Rand reached down and yanked out the vaginal dildo, enjoying the little scream he got out of her when he did. The one in her ass made a wonderful little popping noise as he pulled it out more slowly, listening to her whimper turn to a moan as the tip came free.

He took his time, walking the belt back to the patio and dropping it on her pile of clothes before returning and picking up the hose again.

"No, Rand. I'm serious. No more of that. Really. I can't do this. I'm already shaking."

She was. There was no doubt of that. She was losing control of her body as it responded without her will. He aimed the hose between her legs and turned it on. The water splashed against the tree, hitting the insides of her thighs like so many darts. She jumped just as he expected, spreading her legs wider to keep the water away from her sensitive skin, giving him a perfect shot. Without warning, he aimed higher, the water hitting her slit hard.

Good thing he owned so many acres. Her screech could've been heard in the next county. She turned the air blue with her language and he fought the urge to laugh at her predictable reaction.

Unfortunately, he couldn't keep it trained on her slit more than a few seconds before her dance turned her body away from him, her leg coming up to defend that sensitive spot. Grinning and thoroughly enjoying himself, he turned off the water and made another short trip back to the patio to get the liquid soap and the soft sponge. Lathering her up didn't take long and he could tell by her noises that she didn't care for his rough touch. As though that mattered.

Pouring a generous amount of soap into his palm, he worked it into her hair, knowing that most of the cum would come out but probably not all of it. She squealed again as he managed to get a bit of a lather worked up, his fingers entwining in her normally wonderful rich, brown tresses.

Satisfied that she was marginally clean, he picked up the hose again. In the filtered moonlight, he saw her shake her head, though she didn't protest when he stepped close. Facing the nozzle away from her, he changed the stream to a lighter drizzle and proceeded to rinse her body, using his hands to wipe away all traces of soap. His own clothes, already damp, now got soaked and he decided he should have thought ahead and at least taken off his shoes. Too late for that now.

"Close your eyes and bow your head," he told her before he turned the hose on her hair, rinsing all the suds away. Finished, he turned off the water and threw the hose aside. He undid her left wrist, bringing the right one around to the front. When he held out his hand to re-cuff her in front, she didn't protest. She shivered in the night and meekly gave him her wrist.

Holding her by the cuffs, he led her into the house. First stop, the mudroom. Flicking on the light, he took a moment to look her over.

"You look like a bedraggled cat."

She wanted to make a retort—he could see it on her lips and in her eyes. But her body shivered too much. Picking up a blanket-sized towel, he tossed it over her shoulders and rubbed her dry.

He left her hair in a tangled mess for the moment, not ready to give her back that much in the way of civility. Satisfied that she had warmed up some, he snapped a leash over her handcuffs and pulled her into the house.

The dungeon was just a short trip down a straight corridor but that would allow her to regain her bearings, so he led her in a roundabout route, before coming at last to the ornate door that guarded the entrance to the rest of her ordeal. Pausing to make a bit of a show at getting out the key, he unlocked the door and gestured for Meg to enter. Still glaring at him, she did so and Rand hid his smile. Her anger was right on time. In his experience, anger always followed humiliation. And he'd certainly humiliated her in the club. What had surprised him was how far she'd let him push before starting to lose it. He'd deliberately given her time in the back of the truck to push her buttons even further, programming her anger so she directed it entirely at him.

From here, he had two courses of action, both of which would get her to her breaking point where she faced whatever inner truth she didn't want to admit. He could continue to push the anger, get her really mad at him until she exploded or he could go the softer route—talk with her and explain his purposes. The former ran the risk of going too far and alienating her, the second might defuse her to the point of fizzling out.

The line he chose was a fine one—a narrow fence guaranteed to keep her anger alive, yet prevent her from coming to that breaking point too fast and uncontrolled. He'd walked this fence before with two other subs and learned one major lesson from the experiences—every woman was different from every other woman on the planet. In choosing this path for the two of them, he would be in uncharted territory.

Reaching a decision, Rand toggled a switch on the console, letting soft new-age music flood the dimly lit room. He relaxed his shoulders as the music washed over him, took in a deep breath and let it out very slowly, preparing for whatever bends in the road Meg Turner might throw at him.

Meg pulled the towel tighter around her shoulders, responding to his subtle cues. She found herself relaxing as he did, both body and mind, her anger easing in spite of what he'd done to her. Wanting to stay angry, Meg tried to recapture the frustration and humiliation he'd put her through but all she got was intrigued. She'd never been pushed so far before, either in the challenges thrown at her or in the total control he'd shown both in washing her off and in leading her to the dungeon.

Now he stood before her in soft light, his back to her, his head bowed. Was he gathering strength for whatever he planned to do to her next? Did she have the strength to take more? To her surprise, she yawned, then blinked several times to dispel the sudden wave of weariness that tried to steal over her. What time was it anyway?

Rand turned, his gaze no less intense than it had been outside. She wanted to smile, she really did. Just to show him she wasn't angry at him. But she just couldn't summon the energy to do so. The events of the night had left her too tired.

"Come here, slave." Rand pulled on her cuffed hands, leading her to the corner where the plush rug they'd reclined on before had been replaced by an elaborate wrought iron four-poster. The pillows she'd reclined against last time were now piled at the head of the massive bed. Ornate hangings of embroidered chiffon billowed down from each of the four poles, draping in graceful curves to frame the sides of the large bed — exactly the kind of bed she'd love to burrow into and fall asleep.

Rand stopped her just before the rug to drop the leash and unlock her. She rubbed her wrists, the thin pink lines made by the metal cuffs barely visible in the muted yellow light. With a small flourish and a benevolent smile, Rand pulled back the thick coverlet and sheet. "In you go."

"Oh no...I can't." She shook her head and backed away, even though her heart really wanted exactly what he offered.

"It wasn't a request."

"I know." Meg stood on the edge of the luxurious carpet, her toes sinking into the plush softness. She fingered her still-wet hair with one hand and hugged the towel tight around herself with her other. "I want to, believe me. That bed looks like it would just swallow me up."

"Then what's the problem, slave?"

Meg gave another impatient shake of her head. She wasn't a slave now, she was Meg — didn't he see that? She'd deliberately not used any title for him. "You may have 'showered' me outside but cold water didn't get me very clean. Besides my hair is still wet and that bed is so...so...glorious. I just don't want to mess it up."

Rand dropped the coverlet and stepped toward her, pulling her into his arms. She hadn't realized she was cold until she felt the warm strength of his body encircle her. Sighing, she leaned her head on his shoulder, smiling as she realized her wet tresses would drive her point home by further soaking his shirt.

He brushed the wet hair off her free shoulder, planting a kiss on her bare skin. "You are exactly as I want you to be. And tonight, I want you beside me in that bed."

"Rand, I…" Meg pulled back to protest to his face. She was prepared to fight him on this, to talk him into letting her have a real shower before bedtime or at least an opportunity to comb out the tangles of her hair.

Her words died on her lips, however, when she saw the look of caring and tenderness in his eyes. His hand caressed her cheek as he took her face in his hands, bringing her closer. Of their own volition, her eyes closed as their lips met in a kiss far gentler than she had ever dreamed possible. The kiss of a shadow, the touch of a morning breeze in spring had more substance, more strength. She leaned forward, wanting to feel his lips on hers, her heart suddenly wanting, needing a touch that spoke more of love and longing.

He delivered it to her, his arms encircling her once more, the towel sliding to the floor as she wrapped her arms around him, the world shrinking to this moment, in this small place, inhabited only by the two of them.

She hadn't known he could be so gentle as his tender touch opened a new path to her and her body responded. Slow tingles spread from her center outward as his hands moved over her body, the backs of his fingers caressing the soft skin of her breast, sliding around to her back, past her waist, cupping her cheeks as her lips sought his kisses.

And then they were in bed, their bodies a tangle as nature stole slowly over them, her fingers exploring the muscled curves of his back, his hands pushing her body under his, his hardened cock rubbing against her thigh.

"Oh yes, Rand…please."

"My God, woman, what you do to me. I could make love to you all night."

"Do," she whispered urgently in his ear, suddenly needing his tenderness, his love. "Make love to me, Rand."

He heard the plea in her voice, a plea he couldn't refuse — didn't want to refuse. His lips sought her skin, kissing her shoulder, the hollow of her throat, the swell of her breast. Faint remnants of soap remained from her "bath" and he kissed them away in his sudden desire to please her.

For that was exactly what he wanted to do. He listened to her small moans of enjoyment as his breath heated her skin and his fingers explored, leaving behind trails of longing in her psyche. In the soft light, her skin shone as he slowly awakened her body to passion.

"You are a woman to be savored, Meg Turner," he murmured into her ear, his tongue circling around the outer rim, tasting and probing, feeling her body respond and hearing her whimpers of need.

"I like the way you savor, Rand Arthur," she replied, her voice breathy and uneven.

"Even when I do this?" His teeth caught her earlobe and he pulled, gently at first, then harder when she moaned and moved under him.

"Oh God…especially when you do that." She turned her head as if to get away from him but he didn't let go, keeping her earlobe firmly between his teeth, knowing his breath in her ear drove her mad.

"I'm going to come, Rand. I can't…" Her voice trailed off as his fingers dove to her clit, rubbing and twisting it to push her over the edge. For several seconds, her eyes opened, staring at nothing as her body hung, her breath held lest any movement destroy her bliss.

"Look at me, Meg. Let me see your pleasure."

Her eyes sought his as his fingers moved on her clit and sent her soaring out into space. Of their own volition her eyes started to close.

"Look at me!"

She forced her eyes to his again, not blinking as her orgasm coursed through her body. Her mind filled with him, her body responding as he directed it. No chains bound her, no ropes tied her body, yet a part of her realized she'd been ensnared by something much stronger. Her body convulsed with pulses of heat and she moaned in ecstasy.

He shifted her, turning her on her side away from him, and she was his toy to play with. Her mind still reeling, she turned and when his cock pressed her thigh, she raised her leg, wanting to feel him enter her from behind.

Rand pulled Meg closer, the gift of her orgasm still sounding in his ears. Her flesh, hot beneath his fingers, enflamed him. He pulled her closer, his cock nestled in the fire between her legs.

"My God, Rand. I want to be filled with you."

Meg's fingers reached down to spread her lips wide and guide his entrance. The sweet torture of her touch around the tip of his cock threatened his control but her pussy was close and with a gentle push, he felt her hand fall away as his cock slowly entered her.

Deliberately slow, he kept up the pressure on her pussy, feeling the muscles relent and give way. Her submission to him had been much the same — slow, relentless, determined.

And once fully inside her, he reached for her body, wrapping his arms around her and burying his nose in her hair as she held his cock in her pussy. They breathed in tandem, two spirits joined as one, two bodies entwined together.

But he couldn't hold it long. Desire and passion were even stronger masters than he. With a groan, he moved against her, shoving his cock in and out as her body moved with his. Rand heard their song become one as his balls tightened, ready to fulfill the night's promise.

He held a moment, savoring what lay seconds away before his body crashed into hers of its own accord. In spurts of relief, he came deep inside her as she came a second time, her pussy milking him, pulling from him every last vestige of his orgasm.

And when he lay spent and he felt her snuggle beside him, he had just about enough presence of mind left to reach down and pull the thick comforter over them before he drifted off to sleep, an incredible woman in his arms.

Chapter Seven

✍

Meg awoke in the morning to the delicious smell of bacon frying. She smiled and stretched. It had been a long time since someone had made her breakfast. But the stretching made her realize she slept in the big bed all alone. The lights had been turned up and as her eyes scanned the room, she smiled to think he'd gotten up to make her breakfast.

She heard the lock turn on a small door off to the side that she hadn't noticed before and Meg sat up straighter, a bright smile on her lips. A smile that died when the man who came around the side of the door wasn't Rand. Instead, a white-haired gentleman carrying a tray entered and walked directly over to her.

"Morning, miss. Mr. Arthur has sent breakfast to you, along with some instructions."

Meg had grabbed for the sheet as soon as the older man entered, every nerve suddenly alert at this unexpected turn of events. As he drew nearer, she realized he wasn't nearly as old as she had thought, not with that sprightly spring in his step and a twinkle in his bright blue eyes.

"Who are you?"

"You may call me Mr. Underwood. I am Mr. Arthur's butler."

"Butler?" Did people really still have butlers in this day and age? Where was the guy's English accent if he was a butler?

"Yes, miss. Sit up."

He still held the tray in his hands and Meg realized he meant to put it over her lap. Like Rand's, his tone brooked no nonsense. She looked for a leer in his eyes and saw none. The man was all business but Meg had no doubt every move she made was going into his report to his boss. She stretched out her legs and scooted her rear up against the pillows, still keeping herself covered with the sheet.

"Very good, miss." With a deft snap, Mr. Underwood dropped the legs of the tray and set it over her lap. A simple flourish unveiled an ample breakfast of pancakes and bacon with a dish of strawberries and cream on the side. A tall glass of water and a shorter one of orange juice completed the meal. Meg suddenly realized she was starving.

"Thank you," she managed, keeping her hands firmly on the sheet at her throat.

"You're welcome, miss. I will be back in half an hour to collect the dishes."

The butler crossed back to the door and left without another glance at her. Meg heard the lock turn. She wasn't sure if she wanted to be angry that she was locked in or not.

"Damn." She'd given herself to Rand for the entire weekend, though she wasn't sure she liked being locked in a cage, no matter how big a cage it might be. The warm breakfast scent derailed that thought for the moment, however. She grinned. If being his slave for the weekend included breakfasts like this one every morning, it just might be worth the price of a little freedom. Picking up the small pitcher of maple syrup, Meg drenched her pancakes and dug in.

True to his word, Mr. Underwood appeared exactly a half hour later to take the dishes away. Efficient and businesslike, he made no attempt to touch Meg or to peek under the sheet she once more pulled up to cover herself. In fact, he acted as though her being there, in a basement dungeon filled with tools of torture beside the elegant bed, wasn't out of the ordinary at all.

"Mr. Arthur left this for you, miss." He gave Meg a long envelope as he bent to take the tray from her lap. Meg smiled at him, deciding she liked his kindly face and understated manner.

"Thank you, Mr. Underwood. The breakfast was wonderful."

"If you need the facilities, you'll find them through that door in the corner." He nodded toward a small door in the opposite wall. And without another word, he left, once more locking the heavy main door behind him.

"The facilities", he'd called them. That made her smile. So proper, even if he was as American as she. The envelope wasn't sealed and she flipped it open, pulling out the single sheet of expensive stationery.

```
Slave,


    I hope your breakfast was satisfactory.
Now that you are done, you are to shower and
take care of your toilette. I will be
inspecting you to be sure you are sufficiently
clean, so take care in these matters.

    Should you have need of anything, press
the button on the console marked with a 'B'.
Mr. Underwood will respond. You will not see
me until I have need of you.


    Rand
```

Meg laughed out loud. She dropped her voice in imitation of Rand's. "You will not see me until I have need of you." Giggling she shook her head. "Hollywood, Rand. Very Hollywood."

Bounding out of bed and over to the washroom, she set aside the note, suddenly needing to use the toilet. Not much elegance there. A white-tiled room held a commode, a small sink and a large shower stall. One medium-sized towel lay draped over a steel bar beside the sink. A comb and a toothbrush and paste sat on a shelf just above. "Now, why couldn't he have showered me off down here last night?" she asked the room in general, even though she knew the answer. If he had, she wouldn't have been so humiliated or so aroused.

Taking her time, she turned on the water and gave her body a thorough washing. Scrubbing with soap, she cleansed every last bit of last night's ordeal from her skin. Two latherings of shampoo took care of her hair. Using the towel, she twisted her hair up to get out as much water as she could, then used it to dry off her body. In the end, though, she realized all she did was move the water around as the towel was soaked.

Meg entered the dungeon feeling like a new woman. She'd been fed, she'd cleaned up and brushed her teeth. She could take on the world. Running the comb through her hair, she got rid of the tangles, deciding to explore the room as she did so.

The elegant bed took up less than a quarter of the area, the deep burgundy drapes and sways hanging from the four corners made a romantic picture in an otherwise practical room. Now that she looked critically at it, she realized the wrought iron loops and swirls of the head and footboard had more than decorative purposes. Simply by using a few well-placed ties, a sub could be fastened to the bed in so many interesting poses. In fact, when she stood at the end of the bed and looked at it straight on, she realized the picture created by the curves foretold the bed's main function. One didn't need much imagination to see the double set of handcuffs made by the wrought iron circles.

In the rest of the area, several pieces of bondage furniture held prominent places, their straps and locks testament to their purpose. The high ceiling kept the room from feeling claustrophobic and Meg realized it also afforded Rand room to swing a whip if he wanted. The pulley and chain system he'd used on her the first time hung in the corner opposite the bed, the panel that controlled it on a small stand below. She shivered, pulling a blanket from the bed and wrapping herself in it, though she wasn't all that cold.

A Saint Andrew's cross leaned against the far wall and Meg just passed it by. Although Rand's was better quality, she had something similar in her own room. Jack had fastened her to it often and she was well-acquainted with the sore shoulders that came from being stretched on that giant X.

Next came the rack with floggers, paddles, whips and extra chains, all in their specific spots. She idly ran her fingers through the thongs as she walked past, noting the various textures, from soft and pliable to hard and hurting.

Another console stood near the door. Several rows of levers and buttons controlled the room's atmosphere, from the lights to the music to the air temperature. Tucked in the corner was a small black button the size of a dime, a capital letter B etched in white on its surface. She grinned but didn't press it. Instead she pushed a button to start the CD. Soft jazz filled the room and she let the music play as she continued her tour.

The floor in the center of the room was empty, but a steel grid hung from the ceiling, adorned with various chains and ropes and the odd piece of leather. Rand had spared no expense in putting together this dungeon. From stretching a slave to suspending her, he had an awful lot of toys at his disposal.

The bondage chair he'd put her in last time had been pushed back into the corner, several cages of varying sizes stood in a row beside it. She stood, lost in thought, trying to decide just what kind of man built such a torture room in his house and then hired a butler who didn't blink an eye to walk into it and serve breakfast in bed to the woman his boss had brought home?

A key turned in the lock and Meg was surprised to find her heart jump into her throat in anticipation. Was it Rand? And why did she suddenly want to see him so very much?

Rand saw the smile on Meg's lips as he entered and frowned. Acting irritated, he flipped off the music, though it happened to be one of his favorites. Underwood had been the good cop, now Rand intended to be the bad.

"Over here and kneel." He crossed to the bed and pointed to the mattress. Meg opened her mouth to protest and he saw anger light her eyes. Good. He liked getting her angry. Sooner or later he'd push her far enough that she'd lash out at him and refuse to do what he told her. Until he got her to that point, the point where she'd really do something about the stresses in her life, he was going to push.

Fire in her eyes, she marched across the dungeon and knelt on the bed, the blanket still wrapped around her. He saw the blanket for what it was—a small defiance. He almost smiled. She was only giving him ammunition.

"Put the blanket down and show me your body, slave."

The name he used for her got on her nerves and he could see it. They had no Master/slave agreement. He was her Dom at most. He used the lower term to needle her and he saw that it was beginning to work. Still, she raised her chin and threw the blanket behind her, her breasts pushed out and her body displayed.

God, she had gorgeous boobs. Firm and round, about the size of softballs—too much for even his large hand to encompass, yet small enough that they didn't hang down like overripe pears. The nipples stuck out and it was all Rand could do not to get excited at the very sight of them.

But years of disciplining his mind and body into the ways of a Master, whether he called himself that or not, came to his rescue. Keeping his face impassive, he ran his hands over her shoulders, lifting each arm to check underneath, testing the buoyancy of each breast, then going lower to run his hands over her mound and along the insides of her legs. He might have been inspecting a show horse for all the emotion he displayed.

She rolled her eyes but that didn't fool him. He scented her arousal as soon as his fingers brushed her nether lips. Satisfied that she had cleaned up well, even though he hadn't doubted it, he stepped back.

"Well, you seem none the worse for wear after your use last night."

"Yeah, I wanted to talk to you about that."

"What's to talk about? You gave yourself to me for my use. I used you as I saw fit."

Meg shook her head and leaned back on her heels. "No, not that part. Well, yes, that part but not really."

"You're babbling, slave. Continue to babble and I shall take speech away from you."

She looked up at him in alarm, closing her mouth tightly. Then she started again. "I mean the part about the sex with no bondage. I haven't done that in ages and it felt…nice."

"Nice?" He raised an eyebrow. What was she getting at?

"Being held like that afterward. There was something, oh I don't know… comfortable about it."

"Simple aftercare, slave." If she was going where he thought she was going, he needed to head those feelings off fast. There was a fine line between Dom and sub that was too easy to get tangled up in. And the last thing he wanted in life right now was a romantic entanglement.

The look of surprised hurt confirmed his suspicion. "You've had aftercare with Jack before," he reminded her, driving home the fact that there was nothing more between them, even though his heart lurched at having to be so callous.

"Fine, you lie to yourself if you want but there was more there and you know it."

Rand noted the look of defiance as she lashed out at him and his answer was simple. He turned on his heel, crossed to the pegboard, pulled down a penis gag and crossed back to her. He held it in his hands, giving her more time to dig her hole deeper. For several seconds, she glared at him, waiting for him to confirm or deny her accusation. When he said nothing, he saw doubt creep into his gaze and she was the one who broke the contact.

She looked so dejected that Rand found himself tempted to pull her into his arms, to tell her it was all right, that he had felt something last night and that waking up with her in his arms this morning had actually felt pretty good.

He dismissed that thought and gestured for her to come toward him. With a heavy sigh, she did so, obediently opening her mouth so he could gag her. Once again, Rand realized he'd underestimated her. He'd expected much more of a fight about the gag. But here she was, putting herself one more time into his hands.

Deciding the danger of an emotional entanglement was past, Rand fastened the gag and stepped back to look at her.

"I suspect we peeled away more than a few layers last night, slave. But you have to look further inside. You are nowhere near the center yet."

Meg didn't want to admit it but she knew Rand had her somewhat figured out. There were several more layers to her psyche and, truth to tell, she enjoyed the journey of discovery they took together. But she was sure last night held more promise than just sex and his refusal to admit it ticked her off. Rand retrieved a collar and leash from the wall and she waited with impatience as he fastened the leather around her neck. Three D rings hung at the compass points of her body with the buckle and lock making the fourth. Rand clicked the leash onto the front one. His tug wasn't gentle and Meg scrambled off the bed and followed.

"Stay."

Rand dropped the leash, leaving her in the center of the room. Irritated at being treated like a trained dog gnawed at her sense of self-righteousness and she pushed away the indignation, searching for acceptance. He intended to break down her walls and getting upset wouldn't help either of them. Breathing in deeply though her nose, she let the air out through parted lips around the gag as she sought a place of calm.

He came back with soft leather cuffs to fasten around her wrists. Deciding on obedience, she put her hands behind her back when he told her to do so, even as she looked around the room and wondered just what piece of equipment he intended to use on her today.

But when he opened the heavy oak door and tried to lead her through, Meg hung back. Outside again? In the nude? Last time he'd hosed her down with cold water. She wasn't about to go through that again.

Rand tugged a little harder but Meg dug her heels in. "No, no more water." Or at least, that's what she tried to say. The penis gag made it sound more like, "Nha, nha ma wawa."

Rand stopped pulling and gave her a look of exasperation. "There's a lot to the world other than a little water from a garden hose, slave. Now come." He tugged and Meg warily followed.

True to his word, Rand didn't take her out of the house. Instead he led her through the rabbit warren of rooms and hallways and after a bit, she realized he was giving her the grand tour. She might be naked except for her collar and the cuffs that fastened her wrists behind her but still, he showed her his home. Meg grinned around the gag as he pointed out the technological innovations in the house, including soft music that turned on as they entered a room and faded out when they exited and a set of windows that darkened as the day brightened, then reversed at night to let the moonlight in.

He was so earnest in showing her everything that she forgot about her nudity. The gag prevented her from asking the questions that kept bubbling up but that only served to remind her of her place. As they wandered through the expansive living room and a wide grand foyer, she struggled to swallow around the gag, embarrassed to drool in such elegant surroundings. But as they paused at the foot of a set of sweeping stairs, a thin line of saliva escaped. Throwing her head back, she caught it on her chin and breast.

"Nicely done, slave. I am glad you understand without being told that these rooms have already been cleaned once today."

Everything he'd shown her so far had been on one level — from the dungeon cut into the hillside to the front door off on her left, the sidelights letting in the late morning sunshine. The cooler foyer gave her a chill and she shivered.

Rand gave her leash a small tug again and he led her into the dining room, where Meg paused to take in the incredible elegance of style and design of this room. Where the living room had been large and rambling, it also had a lived-in look to it. The foyer, grand and magnificent in its own way, also had muddy boots in the corner and a jacket thrown over a side bench. Small things that showed the house existed as more than just a showpiece.

But the impeccable arrangement of the dining room set it in a different category altogether. No dust marred the mahogany cabinets tucked under tall windows that let in the morning light. No stray magazine or newspaper lay scattered across the buffet, no left-over dishes from breakfast cluttered the mirrored darkness of the mahogany dining table. The cream-colored walls were unadorned except for one painting that hung over a fireplace at the far end of the room, a painting that made Meg gasp in surprise.

"You like that? It's a Ceriani original."

Meg knew Ceriani, and that he mostly drew sketches for an illustrated erotic magazine called *Snowbound*. But this was no drawing. This was a full oil painting, its colors almost alive, from the translucent skin of the kneeling woman, to the savage control of the man who held her leash. In spite of her surprise, Meg stepped forward to examine it more closely.

"It's called *The Concubine*."

While the dark-haired man stood, fully dressed in nineteenth-century clothing, his face turned toward some distant view, the concubine knelt, her hands loosely bound behind her with rope, her face uplifted to him, adoring. Today's standards would consider the woman plump but her innate sexuality radiated from every paint stroke. This was a woman who had been bedded and bedded often.

Meg's cheeks colored, not because of the eroticism of the painting but because, suddenly and surprisingly, she found herself wanting to be that woman. Could she give her heart so entirely, so devotedly, so passionately, to one man? She couldn't take her eyes from the woman's face, wanting it to be her own.

Behind the gag, Meg tried to swallow as another thought suddenly occurred to her. He had this painting hanging in his dining room. One of the public rooms of the house. Despite the pristine appearance of the room, despite the garden flowers in the cut-glass vase on the sideboard, despite the plush Aubusson rug under the table, Meg realized Rand entertained in this room—entertained in a way very different from other hosts.

She knew, because the rest of the painting put the Master and his concubine into context. A four-poster that looked decidedly like the one in Rand's dungeon sat in the background, its drapes and sways only a shade lighter than the ones covering the bed she'd slept in last night. Another man sat on the edge of the bed, naked, a second concubine eagerly giving him oral pleasure. And in the opposite corner, another woman was bound to the Saint Andrew's cross, her face a mask of ecstasy as another naked man plied her with a whip.

Meg shifted uncomfortably. Damn the man for binding her hands. She would have covered herself, not in modesty but to hide from him the desire that bloomed inside her. The very public display of such a painting and the multiple partners in the painting all combined to send her blood rushing and her desires soaring.

Rand chuckled. "So you like the painting. Perhaps then I should show you its companion." Without waiting for her to nod or shake her head, Rand tugged on the leash and led her through the door to the kitchen.

Homey was the surprised word that jumped to mind. After the showiness of the dining room, she'd expected one of those steel and chrome kitchens with double stoves and giant refrigerators. But Rand's kitchen, though large, combined the welcoming and inviting colors of oak and copper. A long, butcher-block table that extended nearly ten feet along the length of the room dominated the space. Overhead, copper pots and pans of various sizes hung in shiny brilliance. And at the far end of the room, Meg could just glimpse a breakfast nook, the small round table gleaming brightly in an alcove filled with windows and light.

"Good morning, sir…miss."

Meg jumped as Mr. Underwood came in carrying several canvas grocery bags. The man only nodded in her direction, acting for all the world as though having a naked woman, gagged and partly bound, was a totally normal thing to find in his kitchen at eleven o'clock in the morning. Meg smiled weakly behind the gag. Maybe it was. She'd had her share of lovers over the years. Why shouldn't she expect the same thing of Rand?

"Morning, Underwood. I'd like to show Miss Turner the painting."

"Very good, sir."

She still wanted him to use an English accent. There was something mildly disturbing about an American butler. Meg watched him go over to a small control panel—every room

115

seemed to have one of those, she realized — and simply push a button. The wall to her left hummed and parted.

"I keep this one covered to prevent damage from the kitchen grease and smoke. But as you can see, this is where it belongs."

This time her pussy flooded with a sudden need to come. Her knees threatened to buckle and Meg had to lean against the butcher block to keep herself upright.

The revealed painting showed a very different position for the woman she'd seen in the dining room. This time the setting was a dining room and with sudden comprehension, Meg understood it mirrored the one they'd just left. Several guests, male and female, sat around the table laughing, talking, eating. All very normal dining room activities, except for the concubine who lay supine, her arms and legs bound to the table, an array of foods placed on her body. A man on the far side of the table licked what appeared to be mashed potatoes from her mound and another helped himself to the slices of meat from her belly. A woman leaned past him to slide string beans onto her plate. Normal foods in an incredibly abnormal situation. Meg stifled the whimper of need that threatened to give away her thoughts.

"I keep this one in the kitchen as a guide to how a slave should be prepared. Underwood has found it very useful in the past, right, Underwood?"

The butler smiled. "Yes sir. Very useful indeed."

Meg's mind screamed, *You mean you do that? You put a woman on the table like that?* What came out around the gag was the whimper she couldn't hold back. Rand smiled at her, the challenge back in his eyes. "It is how you are going to be used tonight, slave."

She felt herself melt inside, her breathing went deep and her mind momentarily lost focus. When Rand stepped to her and gathered her into his arms, for a moment she simply closed her eyes and imagined herself laid out for all to see — to use. She shied away from the public part of it and yet it enticed her as well.

Rand's finger slipped down to her clit, rubbing it, bringing it alive. Her eyes still closed, she parted her legs and he rubbed harder. In seconds, her whimpers turned to moans as she came in his arms, her body moving against his strength, her mind filled with the image of the painting.

And when she came down and slowly opened her eyes, she looked up at Rand in gratitude, trying to form the words "thank you" around the gag. Rand grinned at her and stood her on her feet once more.

"I think Underwood appreciated your reaction as well." Rand turned toward the butler and Meg's cheeks burned. Now she understood. Rand had put the image of her as a serving platter in her head precisely to get the reaction she had given him. She'd been so taken with the fantasy, she'd forgotten they weren't alone. Blushing, she glanced over at the older man who wore a broad grin on his face.

"Yes sir. This one is very good."

Meg saw the bulge in the man's pants. Butler or no, he was still a man. His reaction both flattered and appalled her.

"Mr. Underwood is uncomfortable, slave. He needs some relief." Rand reached back and undid the gag, gently removing it from her mouth. "Take care of him."

Meg swallowed hard. "You mean…here? Now?"

"Yes, slave. Give him a blowjob. Now."

Mr. Underwood hadn't moved from his position near the console. Her steps tentative, Meg detoured around the large butcher block, her heart pounding. Was she really going to do this? Another total stranger. Had other slaves sucked him before her? Kneeling awkwardly on the kitchen floor, she watched as he unzipped his pants and pushed them down to his ankles. Boxers too were dropped and he presented his cock for her inspection.

The foreskin slid back, exposing a tip that was deep red with his need. The shaft, not very long but very thick, already showed the ridges of the veins under the thin skin. Meg swallowed hard and threw a look over her shoulder at Rand. No mercy showed in his eyes, only a hard challenge. Gathering her courage as a glimmer of understanding came to her, she opened her mouth to take him in.

"Lick him first, slave. You know how to do it."

Part of her just wanted to get this over, part of her enjoyed being used like this. She leaned closer, tentatively touching his cock with her tongue, tasting him first, just as she had first tasted Rand. But where Rand was musky, Mr. Underwood was… well…flavorless. He didn't really taste like anything. She ran her tongue around his cock, pulling it gradually into the warmth of her mouth.

And then he took over. Her eyes went wide with surprise as the butler grabbed her head and simply used her as if she had no other purpose in life but to serve him. Her mouth was there for fucking and that was all she was to him. He slammed his cock into her mouth repeatedly and although she took all of him in, his length didn't reach all the way to her gag reflex. Above her she could hear his deep groan and he pulled out just as he came, his cum covering her face and dripping down to her breasts and stomach.

"Oh yes, she's a good one, sir." Mr. Underwood let go of her head as his hand pumped the last of his cum onto her body. Meg put her head down, trying not to feel revolted by the fact that she was covered in cum for the second time in two days.

"Wash her off, will you? I'll be right back."

Mr. Underwood walked to the sink and a sudden fear stabbed at Meg that he'd turn the kitchen hose on her as Rand had done the night before in the garden. But he only wet a cloth before coming back to Meg.

"Here, miss. Let's get you up." He bent down and took her elbows, helping her to rise. She was surprised at the power the man still had in him. She hadn't tried to guess his age before but now decided he must be near fifty. Matter-of-factly, he wiped the cum from her face, much like a parent would wipe the face of a messy child. Rinsing the cloth, he gave her face another once-over before wiping the drips from her chest and stomach. Meg waited for him to cop a feel while he was at it but the man was all business. In moments, she was clean and dry once more.

"Nicely done, slave."

Why did Rand's compliment give her such a thrill? Shouldn't she be ticked off at both of them for treating her like an object? She ducked her head to hide her smile as she admitted that she actually kind of enjoyed this type of play. In the past eighteen hours or so, she'd given two hand jobs and now a blowjob to complete strangers. Her grin turned to puzzlement as she considered it. Here she was, an independent professional woman with a career—granted, a career she no longer loved but a career nonetheless—being treated as an object for men's pleasure. They didn't know her, didn't care about her. She was used and discarded without a thought.

Her pussy creamed at the idea. No stress, no worries—she didn't need to think or make a decision or come up with a single idea. She simply had to exist and obey. The concept allured even as it repelled.

"Come, slave. I have work to do."

Rand was stymied. He led Meg to his study, the only room in the house designed more for work than play, his carefully controlled demeanor not letting on to the fact that the woman was confusing the hell out of him. After his abrupt treatment of her this morning, he really had expected her to lash out at him. Telling her to give his butler a blowjob was supposed to send her over the edge again, not settle her deeper into complacency. She was throwing his textbook out the window.

He really did have work to do. It wouldn't take long but he didn't want her locked in the dungeon all day. Actually, he did, but he intended it to be as punishment so he could push her buttons even further. But since she hadn't gotten angry, he had no reason to take her back and lock her up again.

She willingly followed him, her eyes curious, taking in the room. He hadn't replaced the gag, deciding her jaws might need the respite. Jaws he'd give a further workout later tonight. Dropping the leash and ignoring her, Rand moved straight to his desk and made himself comfortable as he prepared to get to work. From the corner of his eye, he watched her to see what she'd do.

At first, she did nothing. She simply stood there, her gaze examining the books on the shelves, the leather wingbacks by the fireplace, the leaded-glass windows. The room wasn't huge, Rand liked to keep everything no more than a step or two away to save time when he was in the "zone". The flat-screen monitor on his desk actually was the center of activity here and Rand worked for several minutes in total silence.

"Sir?" He heard the tentative question, also noting that she didn't call him by name. Good. Maybe.

"Yes, slave?"

"May I sit, Sir?"

Ah! A request! Now he had something to act on. He answered quickly and seemingly without thought. "No."

She seemed to take it in stride. After another minute, however, she began to bounce on the balls of her toes. Rand tried not to smile behind the screen as he steadfastly ignored her.

"Do you need to go to the bathroom?"

She stopped bouncing. "No."

"Then stand still."

This time she actually sighed and stood another three full minutes before she began to stretch her arms, first one way around her waist and then the other. He looked at her, although he didn't make eye contact. She stopped, looking irritated and sighed again.

The phone rang and she jumped. Rand turned his back on her as he took the call. Using the reflection of the cabinet behind him, he could still keep an eye on her. She used the opportunity to take a wide stance and bend down, stretching the backs of her legs and her arms as she lifted them up behind her. Because the desk was in the way, he couldn't quite tell how far over she managed to get. Was she limber enough to fold in half?

As his conversation wound to a close, he thought about giving her a verbal head's up that he was about to turn around, then decided against it. He wanted to catch her in something he could use against her and, though this was minor, it was all he had to go on at the moment. Swinging around, he faced her as she came up, her face flushed from her stretch.

She saw his displeasure immediately and backed up a pace. With a combination of rolled eyes and lifted chin, she stepped back where she'd been and assumed a bored expression on her face, ostensibly gazing out the window. Rand wasn't fooled. She watched him as closely as he watched her.

He hung up the phone and addressed her.

"Slave, it seems you have trouble following simple orders. However, I cannot spare the time to take you back to the dungeon just yet. Come here." He pushed back his desk chair but didn't make any move to stand. Still looking irritated, she walked around the end of the desk and stood before him.

"Since you can't stand still, you're going to have to kneel." He gestured to the space under the desk. "Inside."

"What? I can't fit under there!" She stepped away.

He only raised an eyebrow at her. Was this the challenge she would refuse? Waiting her out, he simply sat as she warred with her own psyche. He was almost disappointed when she knelt.

With her arms locked behind her, she couldn't go forward onto her hands and knees, however, so he released her wrists. Patiently giving her an opportunity to rub her sore shoulders, he endured her glares and waited. Finally, she got on all fours and backed under his desk.

But he wasn't quite finished with her. Underwood had gotten a sexual release this morning yet Rand hadn't. Actually, he didn't want to yet but she didn't need to know that. Still, a little pleasure never hurt anyone. He unzipped his pants and pulled out his only partly hardened cock.

"Suckle me, slave. Do not try to make me come," he warned. "I want you to simply hold me in your mouth. This is a gift I give you, the honor of letting me rest in the warmth of your mouth. No tongue, no teeth, just a place to rest. Understood?"

Meg bit back the retort that sprang to her lips. His gift? Who was he trying to kid? And no blowjob—just hold him? In spite of her best intentions, she couldn't stop her head from shaking or her eyes from rolling as she opened her mouth and waited for him to push his chair toward her.

If her attitude ticked him off, he gave no indication. He rolled closer, spread his legs so she could crawl between them and waited for her mouth to encircle him before getting to work. She could hear the click of the keys above her head and the shuffle of the occasional paper.

Like most activities at first, holding him wasn't any more difficult than wearing a gag. But then she had to swallow. He was semi-hard in her mouth—how he stayed that way amazed her. She already knew she liked his taste, so that was a non-issue. And holding his cock in her mouth certainly was a lot more pleasant than wearing a rubber penis gag.

Her mouth tired, however, and the ache in her jaw approached unbearable far more quickly than she thought it would. She really shouldn't be surprised—first the gag, then the butler blowjob—she almost laughed at that. Butler Blowjob sounded like a newfangled drink she should order at the bar. A shot of Jamison's with a side of cum. She couldn't help it, she giggled.

"Something funny, slave?"

She put on a serious face right away and gently shook her head so she wouldn't drop him. A drop of drool slid out of the side of her mouth and Meg ignored it. She'd worn far too many gags to be bothered by a little drool. But then it splashed onto her breast and for some unknown reason, made her giggle again.

He slammed his hand on the desktop. Not hard but strong enough. He didn't pull away from her though. "If you find suckling my cock amusing, I'd like to know."

It was the word "suckling" that got to her. She burst out laughing, dropping his cock in the process. All she could think of were little piglets sucking at their mother's teat. Which meant Rand was the sow. He pulled back his chair to look at her and when their eyes met, she dissolved into fits of laughter, laughing so hard she could barely breathe.

He didn't yell at her but sat there grinning. That didn't help matters. There he sat, in all his glory. His beautiful mane of dark hair a bit tousled from where he'd run his fingers through it as he worked, his body relaxed and leaning back and his now-flaccid cock hanging out of his pants for all to see. Meg collapsed into a heap on the floor, another fit of laughing leaving tears in her eyes.

"Oh my glory, Rand..." She gasped for breath and fanned herself.

"You want to tell me what that was all about?"

Meg shook her head, still grinning. "I'm not even sure. First it was the Butler Blowjob and then the suckling pig..." She lost it again, holding her sides as she tipped over under the desk. "Oh it hurts, it hurts." She grabbed again for breath as her silent laughter made the tears fall.

Rand let her laugh. He liked the sound of it. Not quite the reaction he had hoped for but it would do. Both laughter and tears helped to cleanse the soul, although the latter tended to be far easier to produce. He'd never pushed someone to laughing so hard before. This was a first and Rand decided he liked it. Especially with Meg.

He handed her several tissues and watched her blow her nose and wipe her eyes. Funny how two such opposite emotions could provoke exactly the same physical reaction. And yet the chemicals released in the body were totally different. Weren't they? He'd have to check that out later.

"Better?"

Meg nodded, her breathing returning to normal. She accepted the hand he held out to her and he helped her out from under the desk.

"Good, come over here. Let me just clean this off."

A leather loveseat sat against the far wall, covered with books and papers. He scooped them into a pile and dropped them on the floor, grabbed the lap blanket off the back and spread it over the seat for Meg to sit on.

"I love ya, Meg dear, but I'd rather not get any of your juices on the leather."

Meg chuckled. "Understandable." She sat beside him, not protesting when he put an arm around her. She didn't snuggle but liked the feeling of camaraderie they shared. "I haven't laughed like that in a long time."

Now it was Rand's turn to chuckle. "That was pretty obvious."

She turned to look at him. "Thanks. I really needed a good, old-fashioned belly laugh."

"I don't think you get enough laughter in your life, Meg."

She opened her mouth to protest, then tilted her head as she thought about it. When *was* the last time she'd laughed so hard? Most movies gave her a chuckle but that was about it. Finally she shrugged her shoulders. "I think you're right."

"I liked the sound. I'm just going to have to work on getting it out of you more often."

Meg almost said something, then thought better of it. Rand was her Dom...and becoming her friend. Just like Jack was both Dom and friend. Nothing more. By "more often" did he mean "more often this weekend" or "more often in life"? Several times over the past week she'd found herself thinking of him, of the way his hair curled over his ears or the way that damn dimple got to her. She couldn't be falling in love with a guy who so callously shared her with others. She couldn't be. Could she? Could he?

Hiding her face, lest it betray her, she snuggled into him.

"So while we're taking a break—" Meg started to change the subject but Rand stopped her.

"We're taking a break?"

She sat up, puzzled. "Well, yeah. You're not bossing me around at the moment, so..."

"I *can* Dom without being bossy, you know." He looked positively affronted and Meg laughed.

"I know, except you're not Domming right this minute."

He frowned. "What makes you think so?" He wasn't but he wasn't about to admit it.

"Your eyes." She flounced her hair and settled back into his arms. "When you're in Dom mode, your eyes get hard and humorless. There's an air about you that says, 'don't mess with me'." She paused then added, "Not that you don't always have that air, 'cause you do. I suspect you're pretty ruthless when it comes to your business." With her chin, she indicated the paper-strewn desk. "I mean, you'd have to be. People naturally look up to you and not because of your height." She effectively headed off his defense. She neatly dissected him as if he weren't even there, tolling off his features like a laundry list of qualities. When she fell silent, he prompted her, curious as to where her mind was going with this.

"So how am I different when I'm in Dom mode?"

Meg considered. "When you're in Dom mode, you're…meaner. Your voice is deeper and sharper. You're…well…ruthless. And relentless. You know…a bastard."

The twinkle in her eyes gave away her tease. "You're right on that one. I can be a bastard."

"It's actually all right that you are. I throw as many challenges at you as you do at me. You continually challenge me and I can see the challenge in your eyes. You want to know if I'm woman enough to take what you dish out." She sat up to face him, her tone utterly serious. "And I am, you know. Whatever you throw at me, I can handle."

"Everyone has limits, Meg."

"Yes, and I know we both do. Somewhere. Is it your intent to push me 'til I say my safeword? Is that what this weekend is all about?"

Rand shook his head, "Mostly no. But partly yes." He took her hands, trying to explain. "Part of this weekend is to find your limits, yes. We don't know each other well in that aspect and so we're exploring together. So I'll continue to challenge and you'll continue to accept or, eventually, deny."

"What's the rest of the weekend about?"

"The rest of the weekend is all about pleasure, my dear slave girl." He bopped her on the nose. "It's about exploring sexual passion and having a darn good time doing it." He kept silent about his third purpose—that of getting her to break down and face whatever she was keeping, not only from him but from herself. If it meant crossing a limit in order to make that happen, he was prepared to do that. She'd called him a bastard. If only she knew how close she was on that one.

Chapter Eight

ᔢ

"Break's over. Back on your knees, slave."

Meg heard the tone in Rand's voice change as he slipped back into his role as Dom. With a lingering smile, she slid off the couch and onto her knees before him, eager to find out what new wonder he had in store for her. The laughter had released tensions she hadn't even realized she carried with her and she knelt now with a much lighter heart.

"I'd like to play with that body some this afternoon, slave. See what kinds of noises it makes."

"Yes Sir, I'd like that."

Rand's eyebrow rose. "What you would like or dislike is of no consequence to me, is that understood?"

Meg nodded. She knew otherwise. His seemingly indifferent attitude was all a part of the persona. If it hadn't been, she would've been long gone. "I understand, Sir." With difficulty, she quelled the humor in her voice.

"Good. Because, as much as I'd like it, I do not have the time. Heel."

Without another word, he strode to the door, pausing as she didn't immediately follow. For a moment, Meg thought she'd heard him wrong, that he hadn't just commanded her to follow him on all fours like a dog. But by the way he stood, his incredibly wonderful body framed by the doorway, his finger pointing down to his side, she realized that was exactly what he wanted her to do.

Her leash hung in front of her and with pursed lips, she tossed it over her shoulder as she got on all fours and crawled over to him. Was this really sexy? It didn't seem to do anything for her except irritate. As he moved into the carpeted hallway, she followed, more out of curiosity than anything else. What was this game he played with her? And why, after seeing those paintings, did she suspect it wasn't really a game?

How they managed to get back to the dungeon so quickly she had no idea. Their late-morning tour had done nothing to help her understand the layout of the place. Every time she thought she knew what lay around the next corner, she'd find herself either somewhere she hadn't been yet or in a room she could have sworn should be over on the other end of the house.

Unlike most of the corridors and rooms he'd woven her through, the hallway in front of the dungeon and the dungeon itself were not carpeted. The cold cement floors made her knees ache and by the time he pushed open the ornate door, Meg felt a huge sense of relief. No matter what he had planned for her in there, it would be infinitely better than crawling.

"Stand," he commanded when they got inside, although he didn't look at her. He reached for her leash almost idly with one hand while the other fiddled with the console. The lights grew dim and soft, relaxing music filled the corners of the room. Apparently satisfied, he turned his attention back to her.

"This afternoon you will rest, slave." He eyed her body and Meg shivered to see the lust in his eyes. "Underwood will call for you when he is ready for you." He unsnapped the leash, leaving the collar and her wrist cuffs in place. Turning on his heel, he headed for the door.

"Hold it…" Meg couldn't believe there wasn't more.

"You have something to say to me, slave?"

"Yeah, I have a whole lot to say to you. What game are you playing? You're confusing the hell out of me, telling me the weekend is all about pleasure and then making me crawl here and get filthy on your floors. And then walking out after telling me to take a nap?"

"I want you rested for tonight." His brow furrowed as if he didn't understand her outburst and she relented.

"Oh...well...I just thought..." She gestured to the bed, waggling her eyebrows at him.

Understanding dawned. He came and caught her up in his arms, smoothing the hair back from her face. "Meg. I would like nothing more than to throw you on that bed and ravish you for several hours. Believe me, it's on my list of things to do before the weekend is over." His palms cupped her naked ass, pulling her closer and sending a shiver down her spine.

"But if I do, you won't be in very good shape for our guests tonight and I want you rested, showered and beautiful for dinner."

She pulled back. "Guests?"

"I told you. When we were in the kitchen."

Meg's eyes grew wide. "That picture?"

Rand nodded. "I'm having a dinner party tonight. Six guests and myself. You make the eighth, although you will not be *at* the table. You will be *on* it."

Her mind flashed on the picture in the kitchen. He hadn't been joking. He really meant for that to be her tonight.

"Now get some rest, slave. Underwood will come for you when he is ready."

Her mouth opened and closed twice before she just nodded, stunned. She watched him walk out of the room, then went to sit on the bed, trying to figure out how she felt about being the main serving dish at what looked to be a sumptuous meal.

* * * * *

"Miss? Miss..."

Meg opened her eyes, blinking several times as the room came into focus and she remembered where she was. Startled, she sat up, the locks on her cuffs jingling. She eyed the butler, who smiled at her in return.

"Good afternoon, miss. You are to follow me."

"Yes, yes, I am." Meg had pulled the covers up in an automatic gesture but now ran a hand through her hair and with a big breath, pushed them down. Underwood had seen her naked earlier and soon would be preparing her body for tonight's dinner. What was a little nudity between a woman and her chef?

She threw her legs over the side of the tall bed and stood. The butler handed her an unmarked envelope as he had this morning and she took it from him, opening it to read in front of him when he made no move to give her privacy. Rand's masculine scrawl gave her shivers and a small thrill as she read his directions.

```
Slave,


    I will not see you again until dinner. I
have given you to Underwood, he will oversee
your preparation. I look forward to seeing
your beauty revealed as dinner progresses.


    Rand
```

She folded the note, stalling for time by tucking it carefully back in its envelope. Damn him again. As if being on display for those idiots last night hadn't been enough, now he intended to display her body to a room full of guests? Why was she even considering this?

Because her pussy dampened as she'd read the note, that's why. Because Underwood stood waiting for her, his patient, businesslike manner reassuring her that this was all a test to push her limits. Exactly what Rand told her he would do to her this weekend…and she had agreed. Forcing a smile for the butler, she dropped the note on the unmade bed.

"Well, if we're going to do this, let's get it done."

"Very good, miss. I knew you had it in you. This way."

Underwood's approval gave her a warm fuzzy. Cheered, she followed him into the bath. While she'd slept, apparently someone had been in here adding a few things. A small stool sat on the floor and a red bag hung from the shower rod, a long tube hanging from it, the nozzle end thrown back over the rod. Meg wasn't stupid, she knew what it was and what Underwood was about to do and she balked.

"Hey, I haven't had an enema since I was a kid and got constipated. I don't need one now."

"I'm afraid you do, miss. Mr. Arthur is very particular when it comes to the cleanliness of his serving dishes. You must be sanitized inside and out."

"But…it gets messy!"

Mr. Underwood patted her arm as if she were still a child. "It's all right, miss. Cleaning bottoms is not a chore for me."

"I bet," she muttered under her breath as the butler turned to pull the stool into position.

* * * * *

"Well, my dear Mr. Underwood, that wasn't quite as bad as I thought it would be."

He smiled, never losing his businesslike demeanor as he toweled her dry after her cleansing. "Thank you, miss. You are a stalwart young woman, I must say."

"Thank you, sir."

The butler shook his head. "No, miss. Just Underwood." He finished drying her legs, then held out his hand to help her rise.

"Well, Underwood, Rand should give you a raise for being able to do what you just did." Her mind still reeled with the effects.

Underwood smiled as he straightened the bathroom. "I serve Mr. Arthur in much the same way you do, miss." He turned on the water, preventing Meg from asking the question she desperately wanted to ask.

But Underwood was patient and she could be too. She waited as he set out the shampoo and soap for her shower and when he turned to her, she was ready for him. "Is Rand...Mr. Arthur...is he bisexual?" She had already decided she didn't care if he was but felt she had the right to know. In fact, he should've told her already, just as a matter of honesty.

"Oh no, miss! I didn't mean that." Underwood blushed at her misunderstanding. "Nor am I, for that matter. I meant that I like to serve, to help others, as you do. That's all, miss."

"You were a nurse once, weren't you?" The light dawned and Meg smiled.

"Yes, miss. One of several service positions I have held. But since coming to work for Mr. Arthur..." His voice trailed off and Meg understood.

"Since coming to work for Mr. Arthur, you've found the best position of all."

He smiled happily. "Yes, miss." Underwood gestured to the shower. "All ready for you, miss. I trust you can wash yourself?"

"Yes, thank you. I can handle it from here."

"Very good, miss. Let me remove the cuffs for you." She held out her hands and then put each foot up on the stool so he could unlock and remove the leather bindings. Small pink lines showed around her wrists and ankles where she'd slept on them but otherwise, she was none the worse for wearing them.

"I will be back shortly to take you to the kitchen, miss. The razor is there," he pointed to the sink, "and if you'd rather not shave your pussy, I am happy to do it for you."

Meg shook her head, hearing a faint reluctance in his voice. "I'm sure you have other things you need to attend to. I can take care of that." The time must be near six o'clock and dinner guests would arrive at seven-thirty, with the main dish served promptly at eight. She gave a small shiver as she remembered she was the main dish. Yes, Underwood had much to prepare. She'd do her job and let him get back to his.

Relief shone in his eyes, although his manner never changed. "Very good, miss. I will see you shortly."

With that, the butler turned on his heel, leaving her to her cleaning. Meg stepped into the shower, glad to be alone with her thoughts.

Chapter Nine

ᔡ

Underwood returned with impeccable timing. Meg had just finished shaving the last stray hairs from her pussy when he jiggled the doorknob, giving her a moment's notice before he entered.

"I will need to inspect you before you are allowed in the kitchen, miss." His tone was brisker now, efficient and Meg realized—submissive or not—she was now nothing more than a plate he would use in serving an excellently prepared dinner.

"Of course." She spread her legs a little, feeling a bit of a blush in her cheeks despite all the two of them had been through recently. When he gestured to her arms, she held them up over her head as he walked around her, peering and running his hand over her as if she were a racehorse he considered buying.

"Please put your foot up on the edge of the tub, miss."

She did and he turned her more to the light before bending down and inspecting her sex. His fingers parted the delicate folds and Meg tried to think of unsexy things like winter snowstorms and business meetings but she knew she creamed anyway.

He ran a finger through her slit, gathering the juices she provided, bringing it to his mouth and licking it clean. Cocking his head as if were considering the worthiness of a sauce for one of his dishes, he smiled. "Excellent taste, miss. This will go perfectly with the grilled salmon."

Because he executed one of his butler-sharp turns and walked out, she was left to follow, sputtering. "What do you mean, 'go perfectly with the grilled salmon'? I'm only the plate, right? What—"

Underwood stopped, turning to her with a look of concern. But she realized the concern wasn't so much for her as it was for Mr. Arthur's dinner. "Miss," his voice was gentle yet she detected a slight impatience in his tone. "You are far more than the 'plate'. You are the centerpiece of the evening. Mr. Arthur does not arrange dinners like this very often, I can assure you. You have been given the highest honor he can give you — introducing you to his friends. If you wish to change your mind, then do so now and I will inform Mr. Arthur and arrange to have you taken home."

There was no mistaking the frostiness of his voice. The man took pride in his job and here she was jeopardizing his reputation to prepare a meal beyond compare. Meg shook her head, her voice quiet and repentant.

"No sir. I just...I'm sorry. I thought I was only there to help the display of the food. I didn't know I'm also there to be played with. I didn't mean to upset you."

The butler's shoulders visibly relaxed. "That's all right, miss. I see now that Mr. Arthur is planning surprises for you this evening. Come along." He started to turn away then turned back again. "And just plain Underwood will do, miss." His eyes twinkled and Meg couldn't help but chuckle.

"Yes, Underwood. Come on...let's go make me into a beautiful centerpiece."

Delicious smells greeted her as they entered the kitchen. Pots steamed on the stove and everywhere showed the detritus of culinary industry. What caught her eye, however, was the large butcher-block table in the center, now covered with a long, foil-wrapped board.

"Up you go, miss."

He led her to a small step-stool on the side and Meg gingerly stepped up, sitting her bottom on the board. The foil made small crackling noises as she slid into the position Underwood indicated. Her stomach tight with nervousness, she meekly surrendered each part of her body so the butler could efficiently buckle her arms and legs into black leather bindings attached to various parts of the board.

"We can't have you start when someone accidentally touches a tickle-spot on you, now can we, miss?" he told her by way of explanation. "You need to remain still and the bindings help you do that. Now, test them."

Meg obediently struggled, the foil under her feeling odd as she flattened it hard against the board with the small movements she could manage. Her head, resting in a small plastic bowl of sorts and then strapped down, forced her to stare directly at the ceiling, her chin raised and her neck bared. Her arms had been bound down along her sides, her hands about six inches from her thighs. Her legs had been splayed wide, the ankles bound to the corners of the four-foot-wide board with extra bindings around her thighs to make sure she could not move.

Underwood made some small adjustments to her right wrist and left thigh, then had her wiggle again. This time she had no movement at all.

"Excellent, miss."

"Oooh...Mr. Arthur, he picked a beautiful one this time, didn't he?"

A man's voice, slightly accented, came from over her head and Meg felt her heart jump. A stranger looked at her naked body spread like this! Both excitement and embarrassment made her blush.

"Oh yes. Mr. Arthur found a special one in this slave." Underwood's voice floated from somewhere near the kitchen's stove, his words both comforting and exciting. When he spoke again, he leaned over her to make the introductions. "Miss, this is Raoul, the chef for tonight's meal."

Another face came into her line of vision. Raoul was younger than Underwood but not by much. Probably mid-forties, she guessed, his black hair showing silver at the temples. Kind eyes smiled at her and she liked the way they wrinkled at the creases in his somewhat-plump face.

"A pleasure to provide the cuisine for such a beautiful woman, my dear."

Automatically Meg tried to put her hand out in greeting, forgetting she was caught fast. Unable to even so much as nod, she settled for a tight smile. "Thank you, sir." With her chin free, her voice was uninhibited, even if she could only talk to the ceiling. "A pleasure to meet you too."

"Raoul," the two men said in unison, then Underwood chuckled. "It's a habit she has. But she'll learn. She's a keeper."

Meg gave a slight chuckle, the bindings preventing her from doing more. The butler had such a wonderful way of making her feel good. But then she felt a finger touching her pussy again and her cheeks blushed.

"Excellent sauce for the grilled salmon," Raoul proclaimed.

"That's exactly what I thought," Underwood concurred as he tucked little paper doilies around Meg's body and arranged her hair in a neat fan around her head, taking time to comb it into a perfect half-circle.

The two of them continued to talk over her and Meg slowly realized they had dismissed her as a person. Raoul's only mention of her came when he lamented the fact that he'd been gathering fresh flowers from the kitchen garden when Underwood had fastened the dish to the table. Apparently he liked to help with that.

"Miss?"

Underwood's face hovered into view, only upside down.

"Mr. Arthur would like you to listen to this. This tape will help you to stay still as you are dressed."

She thought the bindings alone were enough for that but didn't protest as the butler slipped an earbud into her ear. He pressed a button on the MP3 player beside her and adjusted the volume, using the set's other earbud. Satisfied, he wiped the bud and put it in her ear.

A soft male voice she didn't recognize told her what was going to happen. "I'm just going to help you relax. That's all I'm going to do. You're going to listen to my voice and go into a nice, deep trance that will help you to relax. You find my voice soothing and comfortable and you want to listen to me as you become more and more obedient and relaxed."

Trance means hypnotism, Meg thought. She'd been hypnotized before at one of those Vegas-style shows where members of the audience came up on stage and then did silly things. It had been great fun and she'd been in control the entire time. Even though she'd known that pretending to drive a car down the highway looked silly to the audience, she had done it at the hypnotist's suggestion simply because he made it sound like fun. She'd also stood like a flamingo and flapped her arms like a great bird at his suggestion, knowing she could simply stop if she wanted to.

The chatter between the butler and chef grew more remote as Meg lay there, listening to the disembodied voice in her head. They didn't talk to her and what they spoke of had no bearing on her life, so she stopped paying attention. Apparently arranged on the board to the butler's satisfaction, she was forgotten. A plate prepared, then left on the table until the meal was ready. She closed her eyes to listen better at the voice's suggestion, letting herself drift and relax.

She felt someone placing something on her belly but couldn't gather enough energy to care. The voice in her head took her deeper and she willingly followed, listening to him tell her how relaxed she felt.

And she was. Keeping her breathing even and unhurried, she found the peace within herself to do this. Rand threw challenge after challenge at her feet. Tonight she would be not only the plate but the sauce as well, having already been tasted and proclaimed perfect by two men. Underwood placed an array of fresh fruits between her arms and body and she didn't even flinch.

Warmth radiated between her legs as he continued to dress her yet she hovered somewhere in limbo, the voice in her head simply telling her she was in no danger and she just needed to stay calm and relaxed as she was clothed for dinner.

She felt Underwood's hands on her breasts, taking one and slipping something around the base to slightly change its shape. The band didn't hurt and when he did the same to the other, she felt him touch her in a detached sort of way. The voice told her she would enjoy being used this way, enjoy being nothing more than an object to be used and she agreed. She'd seen the pictures on the web, she wasn't some neophyte submissive. Rand was objectifying her and she wanted it.

Underwood spooned something warm between her breasts but she couldn't look down to see what it was. If he followed the picture exactly, he filled her cleavage with sautéed mushrooms, dribbling the sauce in artful swirls over her breasts. He teased her open nipples with something cold, which contrasted to the warm substance Raoul spread over her shaven mound.

More warmth on her belly followed as the chef placed the main dish.

Several small bowls were placed around her head, their bottoms resting on her arrayed hair. She had no idea what was in them and didn't care. They were taking such good care of her and all she had to do was go along for the ride. The soothing voice in her head kept most of her attention and she listened intently to his words.

"And now it's time to wake up. You will remember nothing of the events of the past half hour. I'm going to count from one to five and you will awake feeling refreshed and eager to please."

Meg's mind jiggled a little—what was he saying?

"One, two, more and more awake, three, four, nearly awake now. Five. Awake and rested."

With a start, Meg's eyes flew open as the voice fell silent. For a moment, she was confused about what was happening. She remembered Underwood strapping her to the table and vaguely remembered meeting the chef...Ralph? But after that...nothing. She tried to move, only to discover that not only bindings held her down but the weight of the food, artfully arranged around and on her, kept her in place as well.

"Welcome back, miss." Underwood removed the earbuds and took away the player. "The guests are ready for you now."

"But I'm not...I mean..."

"One final touch, miss. Open wide."

Without thinking, she opened her mouth and Underwood placed a small orange in her mouth. It forced her jaws wide, not wide enough to ache but wide enough that her teeth sank into the peel. Juice immediately started flowing over her lips but little of it into her mouth.

"Excellent." Underwood stepped out of her vision. "Now lift her evenly."

Meg felt the board lift, carried by powerful, unseen hands. How many people carried her? How many had already seen her spread like a banquet? Her heart racing, she watched the ceiling slowly move by as they carried her from the kitchen.

Rand watched as the four men carried Meg into the dining room. Underwood had done a magnificent job preparing her, from the small finger bowls arrayed around her head like a crown to the salmon fillets neatly arranged over her stomach. As they set the platform down on the table, Meg's feet closest to him where he stood at the head of the table, he noted the raw carrots arranged between her spread legs to draw the eye to the whipped potatoes that framed her pussy. Rand smiled in satisfaction to see that she already provided a delicious white cream that would go well with everything on the menu.

The men who carried her in were all guests of his and they now came to stand before their chairs at the sides of the table. Two other guests, both male, stood waiting, their eyes shining with appreciation as Meg was set before them, her bound body helpless and designed to please. Orange juice dribbled down her cheeks and chin where she'd bitten through the peel and Rand nodded in approval.

"Gentlemen," he greeted them. "Welcome to this dinner prepared especially for you. I trust you will find her worth the price of the meal. Please, be seated."

He nodded to Underwood and the butler brought over a wine bottle, pouring a small amount into the wineglass. Rand lifted the glass to his nose, savoring the Chardonnay's bouquet before taking a sip to hold in his mouth, letting the flavor build before swallowing it. He smiled. "Perfect."

Raoul and Underwood served many roles in Rand's household, now performing as wine waiters, pouring generous glasses of the vibrant wine for each of the gentlemen gathered. When all were poured, Rand raised his glass in a toast and his guests followed suit.

"To our willing slave and her beautiful body…may it squirm in anticipation and scream in ecstasy over and over and over tonight."

A chorus of "hear, hears" followed.

"Gentlemen…eat hearty!"

As one, they stood to use the utensils at their plates, scooping the sautéed mushrooms from her breasts and taking slices of salmon from her stomach. Several scooped potatoes from her mound to add to their plates before settling back and eating.

The conversation remained innocuous for quite some time as the guests enjoyed Raoul's cooking. Although from different professions, each had many of the same issues with employee relations, the state's regulatory commission and the economy. For the most part, they ignored Meg as they commiserated and congratulated.

The orange in her mouth still dripped juices and one of the men brushed the back of his finger up along her cheek to gather the sticky orange juice. He leaned over her, catching her eye as he licked the finger clean.

Rand smiled and toasted Ed with his glass. He knew he could count on him. At thirty, he was one of the younger members of the group but had gained his admission the hard way. Although he'd inherited his father's air conditioning business, Ed had found the company's books in disarray after his father died. He'd taken over at the ripe age of twenty-six and now had a near lock on providing air conditioning systems for most of the new home development in the surrounding area. He'd brought his company from a one-shop dump to a multi-million dollar business in the space of four years. When, during an extended business meeting, Ed had confided a need for a particular type of sexual release, Rand had brought him into the circle.

He looked around at that circle now. Brad ran an investment firm that dealt with millions of dollars every day. He and his wife were swingers and if she hadn't had a previous engagement Domming another man, she would be here tonight. Seth was in manufacturing—he made canteens and other supplies for the US Army, although right now he was intent on playing with one of Meg's nipples, licking the mushroom juice from it, then pouring a little wine over it before sucking it dry again.

Across from him, Paul went for a different effect, using his fork to gently poke her breast hard enough to leave little pink marks but not breaking the skin. Over and over he prodded, moving around her breast in a random pattern that probably drove her crazy. Under his touch she did seem to try to shift but Rand knew Underwood had strapped her down tightly.

Jeff and Rob dipped into her slit with the handles of their forks, prodding it to continue to make enough juice for both of them. Rob kept slipping the handle in and out but Jeff imitated Paul, flipping his fork around to gently poke at her increasingly sensitive skin before sliding his finger over her clit and pressing down.

Rand simply sat back and watched them enjoy themselves. Meg's pussy continually went into spasms now as they forced her to orgasm over and over. He sipped his wine and smiled. So far, things were progressing right on schedule.

For the better part of half an hour they tormented her, eating the food directly from her body, slurping up potatoes and sauces directly off her skin. Several of the men switched positions at the table so they could sample various parts of her. Ed's fingers reached deep inside her pussy and her body stiffened with yet another climax.

Finally deciding the time had come for dessert, Rand nodded at Underwood and stood. "Gentlemen, I trust your dinner satisfied?"

A chorus of "Yes, very," and "Excellent salmon" met him and he gestured to the kitchen.

"Please avail yourselves of the finger bowls and then, if you gentlemen would kindly clear the table?"

The seven bowls arrayed around her head were passed down along the table. Rand chuckled when Brad "accidentally" spilled some, then had to wipe it off Meg's breast with his napkin. He cleaned his fingers, then nodded to the men.

Ed and Paul took one side, Brad and Jeff the other while the older two men watched them raise the slave to their shoulders and carry her out the door. Rand moved to the sideboard, pouring glasses of port and handing them around, making small talk until the others rejoined them. While part of him wanted to go see how she was doing, he knew that do to so would undo his progress with her so far. He wanted her to break and he was sure serving dessert would do it.

Chapter Ten

ॐ

Meg watched the warm tones of the kitchen come back into view. She had never been so turned on in her life. How many times had they made her come? Ten? Twelve? She had no idea, only that she felt humiliated, used and excited all at the same time.

"Very good, miss! You did excellently well!"

Underwood's voice made her proud of her accomplishment. Although, in all honesty, all she did was lie there, bound and helpless to prevent them from doing whatever they wanted to her, knowing she had given tacit permission earlier, when Rand had shown her the painting in the kitchen and told her that would be her.

She shivered. The painting hanging in the kitchen had become her reality—would the one that hung in the dining room also be played out? From her position on the table all night she'd been able to see only a corner of it. A woman, bent over a railing, her legs spread wide, her arms tied behind her back and a line of men standing behind her, waiting their turn to plunge their cocks into her available pussy and/or ass. The image had pushed her over the edge several times tonight.

Underwood removed the orange from her mouth with some difficulty. In the throes of her orgasms, she'd been unable to move anything but her mouth and as a result, had bitten through the peel and partway through the fruity sections. He wiggled it now as she tried to open her jaw further but the muscles just were too tired.

"No good, miss. You're just going to have to bite through. But don't try to chew what you bite."

With Underwood holding the bulk of the small orange, biting through wasn't as hard as Meg thought it might be. She bit down, feeling her teeth sink into the orange and her mouth fill afresh with juice. He'd removed the band across her forehead that held her down and she raised her head now to let the juice run out rather than trying to swallow it around the large piece she held in her mouth.

Underwood set the section he had beside her among the remains of dinner and reached up to take the remaining piece out of her mouth. The first thing she did was swallow. All night she'd been managing small bits of saliva and juice but now she flexed her jaw and relaxed it for the first time in what seemed eons.

"Here you go, miss. Drink up."

The butler held a straw to her lips and, tilting her head up again, she drank the water he offered. "Thank you," she told him as her head dropped again to the board.

"Very good. Now, we're just going to get you cleaned up a bit and get you ready for dessert."

"Dessert? Like this?" Her head shot up even as Raoul and Underwood released her bindings.

The two men chuckled. "No, miss," Underwood told her. "Not like this."

Relieved, Meg sat up at their direction, letting them wipe her down to get the remains of dinner off her body. Funny how the same movements that, out there had caused her to orgasm, here in the kitchen, were simply clinical. Neither of these men leered or winked at her, they just cleaned her up.

"Over to the shower with you, quick. The guests will want their desserts served shortly."

Raoul pointed to a small door and Meg nodded. Inside was a narrow shower stall with a hose that removed from the wall so she could get to every part of her body. Soaping and washing up, she took a five-minute shower. A tiny table held a single towel and a comb.

She shook her head at her reflection in the small mirror. What would old man Coughlin think if he saw her now? Her smart business suits and professional demeanor meant nothing to those men. Or to Rand, she realized. The play with Jack had always been just that—play. Yes, there had been the underlying current of sexual tension and yes, that had always worked to alleviate her stresses. But this stuff with Rand...

He was pushing her deep into a role she'd never really explored before, that of a sex slave. By allowing strangers, well, strangers to her, to use her, to see her naked, to force her to come... She paused and put her hand on the wall to steady herself before she came again just thinking about it. Taking a deep breath, she corrected herself. By allowing her the choice to be used by strangers, by allowing her the choice as to whether or not she wanted them to see her naked, by allowing her the choice to come or not come at their hands, he gave her an opportunity that had never been open to her before.

And what did that say about her that she had walked right into each of those opportunities with barely a second thought? Was she really a slut inside? Bit by bit, she'd allowed him to strip away the layers of protection she'd built up over the years to keep her heart safe. No one saw the real Meg, not even Jack. And not even Meg looked very often. It hurt too much.

A light knock on the door broke her thoughts. With a final glance in the mirror, she ran the comb through her hair one last time and went back into the kitchen.

The butcher-block table had been cleared, the board stripped of the foil and placed against the far wall. The thick wood table now held various straps and several brass locks. Apparently she was going into bondage again. Her smile tight, she came to stand in front of Underwood. Raoul was nowhere to be seen.

"Turn around, miss. I will dress your hair."

"With what, whipped cream?"

She hadn't meant that to sound so sarcastic. It wasn't Underwood's fault that she allowed Rand to push her so far. The image from the dining room painting flashed in her mind again. Did he really intend to push her that far? And if he did throw down that challenge…did she have the courage to pick it up?

Underwood only smiled at her as he braided her still-wet hair into a neat French braid. When done, he told her to put her arms behind her back and when she did, he slipped the burgundy armbinder over her arms. She'd worn this the very first time she and Rand had played. The familiarity brought a small comfort as the butler tightened the laces that prevented her from bending her arms.

Last time, however, Rand had fastened the fingertips of the binder to a belt that he ran down between her legs. Underwood had no such belt attached to the end this time. He bent down to attach sturdy leather cuffs to her ankles, locking them in place, and Meg took a deep breath, allowing her mind to sink down into the bindings, exploring the small movement her arms still had, reveling in her inability to escape. The ball gag he put in her mouth next settled her even further.

Now he picked up a small tray, two straps and two chains hanging down from it. The straps he fastened around her waist, pulling them snug and buckling them tight. The tray dug into her belly a little, the far end tilted downward. He came around front just as Raoul reentered the kitchen, a tray of crystal parfait glasses filled with the layered dessert. When he set the tray beside her on the butcher block, Meg's heart jumped. Surely they didn't mean…

Underwood, with a chain in one hand, now pinched her nipple with the other. "Small pinch, miss." Quickly he attached the clamp to the base of her nipple and she breathed out through her nose at the sudden rush it gave her.

"And again." He fastened the other clamp and the tray now lay perpendicular to her body.

"You'll make two trips, miss." Underwood explained her duties as he gently set first one, then the second and third parfait glasses on the tray before her. The weight of the first one wasn't hard to take but the second and third stretched her nipples until they were painfully tight.

"Go now, miss. And do not drop them." She heard the warning in his voice and decided she didn't want to know what the punishment would be for embarrassing Rand in front of his guests. He trusted her to do this. Or at least, Underwood did.

The butler preceded her, opening the door and announcing that dessert was served. She kept her steps small, the little locks on her ankles barely jingling as she carefully made her way into the dining room. Unsure which guest to serve first, she hesitated just inside the room.

"Excellent." Rand's voice boomed from the other end of the table. "Slave. Serve the right side of the table first." He gestured and Meg realized he meant his right, not hers. Starting past Underwood, she paused again as the butler murmured, "Serve from the right, take away from the left." Nodding slightly to let him know she heard, she continued.

The men continued their conversation as if she weren't even there, although every one of them followed her with his eyes. Were they waiting for her to trip? To tip a glass over? Determined that she could do this and do it at least with a margin of grace, she moved to the right of the man at the foot of the table. When he lifted the glass from her tray, she tried not to moan in relief. Who could have known one simple dessert glass could weigh so much?

Going around to the second man was a little easier with the middle glass gone. But when he took his dessert, the tray was no longer balanced and Meg had to adjust her posture quickly to avoid dropping the remaining glass into the lap of the man on her left. Bending a little to the right, she backed up and moved over to the man's right, where he took the dish from her.

Now she did let out a relieved sigh. Throwing a quick glance at Rand, she felt grateful at the glimpse of pride she saw in his eyes before the look changed to a stern one when she didn't move fast enough to get the remaining glasses. She would have smiled around the gag but her nipples ached and she really wanted these clamps off.

Raoul stood in the doorway, the remaining desserts on a tray before him. At least she'd be saved the walk back into the kitchen. She stoically accepted the first two glasses as they again stretched her breasts out. The third made her whimper in spite of her best intentions and the fourth and last one brought tears to her eyes.

"You're doing fine, miss." Underwood's muttered encouragement helped her to turn toward the guests, who had fallen silent and simply watched her. If she'd looked, she would have noticed several of them were rubbing their cocks inside their pants. Her travails had made them hard. But she was intent on making it to the table without incident and didn't have any extra energy to spend looking around the room. She had one target, the man at the near end of the table.

Stepping to his right, she waited as he removed his dessert, his gaze never leaving her stretched breast. Backing up again, she moved to the man in the middle, grateful for the release in pressure as he took his glass. Two more and she'd be home free.

She should've known by his leer that the last guest along the side would be the most difficult. Not content with simply reaching over to take the dish from her, he made sure his fingers brushed against her sore nipple as well, sending a wave of pain coursing through that sensitive bud. Her intake of breath, audible in the quiet room, made several men chuckle.

And as if that weren't enough, he pressed down on the glass, pushing the tray down and stretching her until she bent from the strain. But that sent Rand's dish sliding toward the edge and she was forced to stand up again and bear the pain.

Now several of the men laughed outright and the guest beside her suddenly released his pressure, lifting his parfait to set it on the table before him. The release made her step back to keep from overbalancing as Rand's dish once again slid on the tray. Tears formed in her eyes, partly from the pain but more from embarrassment. Throwing a glance at Rand as she came around the end of the table, she let him know she didn't think much of that particular guest.

But if she expected sympathy from him she didn't get it. He took the last dish from her with a simple instruction. "Remain there, slave, until it is time to clear."

Meg nodded, a small tear sliding down her cheek. Her nipples truly ached now, the slightest movement sending darts of pain ricocheting around inside. While this had been fun at first, she slid past that point now and the cream that had slid down along the inside of her thighs dried in the cooler dining room air.

Thankfully, they returned to their conversation and left Meg to her own thoughts. She tried to follow along at first but the names they threw around meant nothing to her. Finally she realized they were talking about baseball teams and she tuned them out entirely.

Of course, without their conversation to keep her mind off things, all she could focus on was her situation. So far she'd been a plate and a serving tray tonight. Two objects. Nothing more. Yes, several of them had enjoyed giving her orgasms while she'd been locked down and unable to prevent them but that didn't count. She didn't exist as a real person to them. She was just a plaything.

And how did she feel about that? Surprisingly, she felt fine with it, Meg realized. Being an object was an almost welcome relief from the day-to-day business of running a huge department where she made hundreds of decisions every day. From deciding which pieces would be on the front displays to dressing the manikins in the latest fashions, it was her responsibility to make decisions that would make the company money.

And now she was no more to these men than the manikins were to her. Her cheeks colored slightly as she remembered Rand's puppet machine. That had been his first use of her as an object. With sudden understanding, she looked at him, sitting comfortably at the head of the table, not really joining the conversation, only putting in a word here and there to direct it. That was it! He directed the men here much the same as he directed her.

From the first moment she met him she'd understood he would reveal only what he wanted her to see. Except now she'd cracked a little of his shell. He was in charge at every turn, in every situation.

Which left her, precisely, where? Rand finished his dessert and put his empty dish on her tray without thought. Or seemingly without thought. He pointed around the table and her orders were clear. "Take away from the left," Underwood had told her. But the jerk on her right didn't show any signs of wanting to get rid of his dish. She was saved having to make a decision by the man on Rand's right who crooked his finger at her and winked.

An object for them to use. The thought ran continuously through her mind as one by one they placed their empty crystal dishes on her tray. She collected four, looking at Underwood when she got to the end of table. The butler gestured her over and removed the load, then nodded to the table for her to finish clearing.

Her breasts truly in pain, she turned to gather the last remaining dessert dishes. The tears she'd fought back before now gathered again as two of the guests put their dishes on her tray at the same time, the sudden weight proving hard to handle. All that remained was that last guest, the one who had given her grief before. She came to stand at his left, silently waiting as he continued telling a story, totally ignoring her presence.

The tray grew heavier, each breath making it rise and fall, each breath becoming a private pain as a result. Her lip quivered against the red rubber gag, drool dripping down her chin to land on her stretched breast. As if floating in another sphere, she watched his hand reach for the parfait glass, raise it and set it surprisingly gently on her tray. Giving a mental sigh of relief, she turned and took the dishes to Underwood, who again took them from her at the door.

"Remember, miss. Big breath in."

She didn't have time to ponder his words as Rand called her back to his side as soon as Underwood removed the last dish.

"By my side, slave."

Part of her wanted to tell him where he could put that word. She was getting damn tired of it. Underwood had shown more feeling, more understanding than her chosen Dom. Maybe she played with the wrong guy. Despite their age difference, she liked the butler. The "Master" was getting on her nerves.

Still, she walked over to where he sat, the tray still hanging from her now-swollen nipples. He stood, pushing his chair back from the table and turning her so that she faced the gathered guests. Several of them rubbed themselves openly, sitting back in their chairs, one hand beneath the tablecloth. No way was she going down under there tonight, Meg decided. Once was enough for that.

Rand slipped behind her, undoing the belt at her waist and letting the leather straps fall. Then with a quick movement, he pushed the tray away from her belly so that it laid flat, the weight of it suspended entirely from the clamps at her nipples.

The action took Meg by surprise and she couldn't control the moan of pain nor the need to bend forward. But the instinctive movement didn't bring her relief, in fact, it did just the opposite. Rand took care of that by using the tail of her braid to pull her back upright.

"Let's get rid of that tray, shall we?"

His hand touched the clamp at her right breast and she leaned against him as the torture threatened to overwhelm her. Remembering Underwood's admonishment, she took in a deep breath and nodded. With a quick gesture, Rand removed the first clamp.

The pain was excruciating. She, who prided herself on her composure, who took great pains to keep a stiff upper lip on all occasions, cried like a baby in front of all these powerful men. Turning her face into Rand's shoulder, she knew there was worse to come. He held the chain in his hands so the entire weight didn't hang from one tender nipple but in a few moments, that wouldn't matter.

"One, two," Rand counted softly in her ear so she could gather her breath. "Three." He released the clamp and if he hadn't been there with his arm around her waist, she would have fallen to the floor. Handing the tray off to the butler, he turned her to face him, one arm still around her waist, the other massaging both breasts as the blood rushed back to the tips.

"Turn, slave, let them see your face."

Humiliated, the tears still streaming down, she turned to face the men at the table. One of them had come around from the other side and now stood near her. Rand helped her. "Kneel before him, slave. Show him your tears and give him satisfaction."

Meg sank to her knees, grateful to not have to stand anymore. But as she looked up at the now-exposed cock of the man before her, her tears continued to fall in embarrassment that they had all witnessed her breakdown.

"Look up at me, slave," the guest's rough voice commanded her.

She did, her lips trembling around the ball gag, sniffling and praying he didn't want her to suck his cock. He didn't. Already the man's eyes were unfocussed and with a grunt, he came on her face and breasts, large gobs of stringy cum mingling with her tears. Meg couldn't help it. She didn't like it and she turned away. Only Rand's hands on her shoulders kept her from pulling back entirely.

Finished, the man looked down at her, still kneeling before him. "Your shame and humiliation are a great aphrodisiac, woman. Thank you." He took the damp cloth proffered by Underwood and wiped his shrinking cock, tucking himself away before returning to his seat at the table.

"Seeing a woman humiliated and used gets me going too."

Meg tried not to show disgust for the man who had spent the night at Rand's left and who had caused her so much anguish earlier. After a glance at him, she turned away and the men's laughter rolled over her head.

"Oh Rand, you've got a spicy one here. She was so pliable on the table that I didn't realize how hot she could be when given back some freedom."

Meg steadfastly refused to look at the guy who had hurt her before or to take the bait. But when he leaned down from where he sat in his chair and put his lips near her ear, it was all she could do not to shrink away at his words.

"I, for one, will enjoy watching you being brought down a peg or two tonight, my lovely." His fingers pinched her sore nipple. "And then you will beg to wear the present you currently despise."

This idiot got her dander up. She flashed him a look of pure malice only to have him laugh again. It didn't help when Rand allowed him to help her up, each of them on one side of her.

"Shall we adjourn to the library?" Rand gestured and Underwood opened the door to the hall. As she passed him, he winked at her. Meg almost smiled. The butler's confidence in her did a lot to bolster her courage. Whatever her bastard of a Dom could dish out, she could handle.

The first guest's cum had dried on her skin by the time they crossed the hall to the plush and comfortable library. Rand hadn't shown her this room before. Larger than his study, the room looked like it belonged in a men's club. Leather couches, a thick oriental rug on the floor, heavy curtains that shut out the late spring night and a large fireplace at one end all combined to give the room a sensuous feel. Because the weather was warm, a screen decorated the front of the fireplace but from this end of the room, she couldn't quite make out the picture on it. Knowing Rand, it would be something lewd.

The glass-fronted bookcases that lined two of the walls were raised, however, and she found that a curious feature. One had to step up onto a platform to get to them. A railing ran along the platform and several of the couches and chairs backed up to it. Her eyes widened in shock as she looked again at the railing. The same pattern as the railing in the dining room painting twirled and dipped in sensuous lines. The same railing the slave had been bent over, tied down to while the men waited in a line to use her. Was that what Rand intended for her tonight? She looked at him in panic.

But he had left her standing near the door while he continued into the room. Each man, as he passed, touched her in some way, almost as if she were a good-luck charm or something. While several of the touches were accompanied by appreciative glances, more than one just touched as if out of habit. She meant nothing to those men. To them she was simply a piece of the furniture. Meg wasn't sure if she preferred that or not.

Her relief was short-lived, however. The last one in, the idiot, shut the door and his leer made Meg realize that this one, anyway, fully intended to fuck her before the night ended. Over her dead body, she decided. The other men she didn't mind. Even the guy who got off on seeing her crying in pain was okay. At least he wasn't slimy. He knew what he wanted, got it and masturbated to it. She was surprisingly okay with that.

But this idiot just rubbed her the wrong way. She didn't like him and she hated the fact that he thought he could lord it over her. Who was that character in *Pretty Woman*? Richard Gere's friend who thought, because Julia Roberts' character was a hooker, he could have his way with her? That was this guy. That idiot in the flesh.

The men discussed something in quiet tones, over by the fireplace, but Meg couldn't hear what they said. That was fine with her. She was perfectly willing to stand here as statuary while the idiot joined them. Whatever they were talking about kept them occupied and all she had to do was stand here and hope they would forget she existed.

Chapter Eleven

ॐ

Rand chuckled as his friends oohed and ahhed over his slave. This wasn't the first dinner they'd participated in but certainly was proving to be among the most memorable.

"That was excellently played, Rob. Coming on her like that?"

"I wasn't sure if you'd allow it, but damn, seeing a woman's tears like that always makes me hard and ready."

"I'm glad you did. Well done."

Jeff came up to join them. "This one's full of spit, Rand. I know you said you wanted to break down her defenses tonight but I'm thinking maybe I should leave. I only seem to get her mad."

Rand shook his head. "No, I have to admit, I thought I had her with the dessert. Figured the pain in her nipples would make her break and it did but not far enough."

"This one's tough. I'm betting two hundred dollars our Rand has met his match."

Paul's bet hung in the air. A moment later, they were all reaching for their wallets.

"You're on."

"I see that bet."

"I'm putting my money on the girl."

"My money's on our boy here."

Rand laughed and threw his own two hundred into the pot. "I think only Ed and I are going win money tonight. Thanks for the vote of confidence, pal."

Ed grinned as Paul collected the money and slipped it under a book on the fireplace mantle. "Just don't let me down, buddy. I have my eye on a certain set of nipple diamonds for my gal," Ed said, chuckling.

"Okay, I'm going to push her further. I let her have her safeword this weekend because I knew it would make her feel better. But she hasn't used it yet and I'm thinking she's just stubborn enough not to use it. We need to get those barriers down a lot further. I'm thinking a good flogging and a whole lot more forced coming should do the trick."

Brad flexed his arm and said, "I could use the exercise. How hard do you want it?"

Rand knew exactly what he wanted. "Lull her first," he instructed, "then raise the level. Let's see what she can take, shall we?"

"I call coming all over her flayed back!" Ed rubbed his hands together in anticipation.

Rand laughed, clapping Ed on the shoulder. "You got it!" He took a deep breath. "Ready, gentlemen?"

The smiles around him deepened as their demeanors changed, each one settling into his own Dom mode. Rand walked back to his waiting slave, the men drifted apart, one going over to pour another glass of port, several to recline on the couches while Brad went to a closed cupboard to the side of the fireplace to choose from among the floggers he knew would be there.

Rand walked up behind Meg and unbuckled the small rubber ball gag. She stretched her mouth and swallowed several times and he just waited. At the precise moment he knew it would bother her most, he told her, "Come, my guests wish to hear your screams."

He cut off any protest she might have by grabbing a nipple and pulling her along, forcing her to follow. Her mouth still hung slack where first the orange and then the ball gag had stretched her jaw muscles and gotten them used to being open. Soon she'd regain control and her mouth would work just fine. In the meantime, he intended to, to put it crassly, fuck with her mind.

Ed and Jeff moved a couch from against the railing, turning it so they would have a good view of what happened up against the wrought iron work. Rand led Meg into the middle of the area they'd cleared, leaving her alone and the center of attention.

"Rob, take off that armbinder, will you?"

Rob was happy to oblige, making sure he pulled up on the laces so that she had to bend forward, her breasts hanging down for their amusement.

"I like the tits on this one, Rand," Jeff said. "They're just not big enough. Give her a boob job and she might make a passable piece of ass."

Even from where he stood beside Brad, Rand could see the anger flash in her eyes at Jeff's rude remark. Good. Jeff was a good friend and they'd Dommed together several times in the past. Rand understood that Jeff had seen her respond to his slimy behavior and that he kept it up now to push her further toward a breaking point.

"That's a good idea. If this one's worth keeping around, I will consider that."

Her head snapped around to look at him, obviously stung by his words. Okay, that surprised him. What was she reacting to? The insult? Or the keeping around idea? Rand turned away, not wanting her to see his puzzlement.

She was his sub and he was her Dom. That was it. Right? They were nothing more to one another. He didn't want entanglements and neither did she. That was why they were such a perfect match. This whole weekend was just about getting to the root cause of her stress and helping her to deal with it. He just had to get her to break down enough, confess what really bothered her and face it. Then he'd help her find a way to deal with it and they'd be done.

Only why did he feel like he'd suddenly wounded her far more deeply than he'd intended?

Rob wrapped up the armbinder, Meg ignoring them all as she stretched her arms in front of her. Rand nodded to Paul, his mind still whirling even as the man took her wrists and led her to the rail. Seth and Ed stood on the platform, leather cuffs ready to lock around her wrists. The leather wraps for the ironwork were already in place. A simple snap and her arms were locked above her head and out to the side. Below, Paul and Jeff helped her to spread her legs wide, locking them into strong rings embedded in the side of the platform. He'd outfitted more than one room in his house for playing with a slave.

"Gentlemen, if you'll all take a seat, I'm sure my slave would love to perform for you."

Rand took one of the armchairs to the side where he could watch her face. If this pushed her over, he wanted to know the moment it happened. Judging from past encounters, however, he doubted a simple flogging would be enough. But it would send her further down the path he crafted for her and that would do.

Brad had chosen two floggers—one for each hand. He began with the soft one. "Lull her," he had said. Rand relaxed. Brad could wield anything from a light flogger to a bullwhip with precision and ease. In fact, he'd won several competitions with his ability to make a whip do what he wanted. She was in good hands.

At first she showed little reaction to the light blows but then her shoulders suddenly relaxed as if she'd decided that she might as well enjoy this. Having this done in front of others disturbed her, Rand knew. But the fact that she'd come so many times on the dining room table told him at least one part of her enjoyed the exhibition. Apparently that was the part of her that had taken over now.

The blows became nearly imperceptibly harder across her shoulders and ass. Rand approved. Brad was a master at this.

The heavier blows across her shoulders turned the skin pink but she remained still, simply accepting the leather's caress.

Brad added the other flogger, landing the blows at double-time now. The second had stiffer thongs and left more of a sting, which the softer one in his right immediately caressed.

Finally she moved. Not far, her bindings didn't allow for that. But a small movement followed a moment later by a whimper. At Rand's nod, Brad dropped the softer flogger to the floor, switching the harder flogger into his right hand without losing a beat. A moment more and Underwood had retrieved the unused flogger, set it on a side table and picked up a four-foot-long single tail that Brad had set there. Underwood held it ready for when Brad should call for it.

Silently Rand blessed whatever force had sent Underwood his way. The man had proven to be an invaluable find. A natural submissive in life, he was the type of man who, upon being given a job, would see it through every detail to completion. Speed wasn't important, meticulousness was.

Underwood had admitted he wasn't much of a sexual being. The occasional blowjob would suffice and Rand had readily agreed, knowing the women he brought home wouldn't mind. And those who did, well, that was certainly a deal breaker for him and only once had that happened. He'd promptly given that woman back her clothes, shown her the door and, by the end of the day, had set her up with a Dom more her style.

Meg shifted more in her bindings, the whimpers turning to moans as her skin grew a darker pink. Brad had moved down to her thighs, giving her entire body a workout. Rand made a gesture and Brad grinned, changing the aim and force of the next blow to land on her pussy lips.

She cried out, more in surprise than hurt, Rand knew. Brad landed more there, the thongs of the flogger turning dark with her desire. She rested her head on the iron railing and her hands balled into fists as her need climbed. Each blow brought a whimper or small cry of need and Rand indicated to Brad to pick up the pace.

Across the room, Seth nudged Ed, who had his cock out, rubbing it in anticipation. Nodding to the platform, Ed grinned and stood. Together they moved to stand in front of her on the platform, both their cocks out where she could see them.

"Open your eyes, slave. See what your performance has done."

The flogger between her legs didn't let up but she opened her eyes, another cry escaping as she saw the two cocks poised. Pre-cum dripped from their tips.

"Come, slave," Rand's voice rang out. "Come for them. Let your cries feed their need."

Brad's tempo increased again and under the onslaught, she had no choice. Her body arched and quivered in her bindings, her cries filled the room with her need. And when she screamed out her orgasm, both men came, groans mingling with her cries, their cum spurting down to cover her writhing body.

From the sidelines, Jeff applauded the spectacle, slapping Brad on the back and congratulating him on a job well done. Underwood silently approached the two men on the platform, handing each a wet, warm towel to clean their cocks. Rob came to stand beside Rand.

"I do like the noises this one makes," the older man told Rand. "When you tire of her, send her in my direction. I'd love to hear her entire range."

Rand grinned. "Oh believe me, she can make some pretty ugly noises too. You haven't heard her in a bad mood."

Brad moved to put away the floggers and now turned to join the conversation. "I can whip that bad mood right out of her if you want, you know."

"Grab that single-tail." Rand's chin jutted toward the cubicle that held some of his finer instruments. "Show me."

Up above, Seth and Ed finished cleaning themselves, giving their towels back to Underwood and tucking their satisfied cocks back into their pants. Reaching forward, they unfastened Meg's cuffs from the railing, giving her an opportunity to once again stretch her muscles. Down below, Paul released her ankles and Meg turned to face the room. But that allowed Ed and Seth a good look at the cum drying on the reddened skin of her back and she had to endure their high-fives and congratulatory remarks to one another.

Rand stepped in front of her, taking her chin and tilting her head up so he could see into her eyes. Her jaw clenched pretty tightly but her eyes flashed neither defiance nor anger. She was tiring, yet had more to go through before he would let her rest. Abruptly dropping her chin, he turned away with a simple command. "Come."

He walked to an old roll-top desk, pulling the lid firmly down before pointing where he wanted her to stand in front of it. Rob stood to one side of the desk and as Meg turned her back to the roll top, he took her wrist. Rand did the same and they bent her back. Her eyes flew wide as she realized what they intended, adjusting her stance and spreading her legs to keep her balance as they fastened her cuffs to the back corners of the old-fashioned desk. In short order they attached her ankle cuffs to two small eyehooks in the bottom corners and she was caught, her body spread and open, the sensitized skin on her back and ass pressed against the wooden slats of the closed top.

"Now let's see what that four-footer can do." Rand and Rob both stepped away as Brad came over, a long single-tailed whip in his hand. The frayed end provided a somewhat softer sting yet Rand knew from his own experience that not only would the tail leave some very nice stripes but that those stripes would hurt.

Brad needed room to swing and the men moved to the side where they could watch and not be in the way. Jeff stepped up to the bound slave, however, before joining them.

He leaned in, his fingers lightly running up from her navel to her breasts. The nipples, still pink from their earlier use, stood out and he simply brushed the backs of his fingers over one, his hand coming up to trace her jawline. With every movement of his hand he showed her just how vulnerable she was to him.

"You will beg to have me come on your striped body. Your breasts will wear my present to you—after you beg."

You're an asshole as well as an idiot, she wanted to spit at him. But, over his shoulder, she could see Rand and Underwood waiting at the fireplace. Disappointing Rand she wouldn't mind. This asshole pushed her close to her limit. But Underwood? He had so much faith in her. She could do this. For herself as well as for the butler.

Meg didn't reply, keeping her gaze on Brad and the whip. Jeff nipped her earlobe with his lips and moved away and she let out the breath she'd been holding.

Her fingers balled into fists as she held herself ready. She saw the man draw his arm back, saw the casual flip of the wrist and the follow-through with the arm. For a moment, she thought he'd taken a practice swing. But then a hot knife of pain slashed across her stomach and she lay her head back on the wooden desk as a second slice cut through her exposed belly. Her chin quivered and she gritted her teeth. She wouldn't cry out. She wouldn't give them the satisfaction. A third cut left its line of pain and she twisted away from it, knowing she couldn't take many of these.

The next crack slashed across her breasts, leaving a thin pink line searing her skin. Even then she tried not to make a sound, the small cry forcing its way out in spite of her best efforts. He whipped her breast again, the tiny tail marking her skin in its wake.

"Breathe, slave."

She heard Rand's voice like a clarion showing her safe passage. With a rush, she let out the air she'd been holding, grabbing a huge lungful of fresh air. As she breathed, her head cleared a little and she realized the stings still ached. Unlike before, where the sting went away after a moment, these tended to linger. She opened her mouth to say something to Rand, when another blow across her breasts sent the thought flying out of her mind.

The strikes were becoming harder to bear. She squirmed in her bindings continuously now, wanting the whipping to stop. Her mouth formed words but she had no idea if any sound came out. All she felt was pain as he brought his hand back and sent the end of the tail sliding across her sensitive skin.

"Beg for Master Jeff's cock, slave. Beg to wear his cum."

She looked at Rand through her haze and shook her head no. Damn fool. He's a damn fool and she wasn't going to beg and give in to his ego. Whose ego? Another crack of the whip opened another trail of fire. Rand's? Master Jeff's? Her own? Who was the damn fool?

Meg broke, tears streaming down her face. Being flogged had been pleasant compared to this. She could come from the flogging. This just sent her mind in a fast retreat away from the pain.

"Beg, slave."

"Shit. I don't want to!" She didn't even realize she screamed her answer.

"And do you think I care about what you want? Do you think that matters to me one tiny bit?"

She knew it didn't. And yet it did. It did matter to him and he pushed her anyway. The small part of her brain that still held to rational thought understood he pushed her. But where to? Was he going to push until she refused? Or push until she gave in? She was here to relieve her stress...wasn't she? Then why did she find herself wanting to go further? Wanting to push her will against his in this struggle?

The single-tail moved from her sore breasts, slicing lower and lower on her front. He slashed across her thighs several times and Meg sobbed. What was she supposed to do? What did Rand want from her? Acceptance? Or stubbornness? And more importantly, what did she want? Did she know anymore?

And then the whip landed on her sensitive nether lips, a light sting meant as a warning. In panic, Meg's eyes flew open and her head came off the desk as she stared at Brad.

"No, please. Don't. Not there. I can't take that. Please don't." She looked at Rand in total panic.

Rand simply crossed his arms. "Then beg to wear Master Jeff's come, slave."

For a moment, she held her own, her eyes searching for her answers in his eyes. The rest of the room faded from her thoughts as she struggled. Rand turned away from her and made a gesture to Brad, who brought the whip up to set another light sting on her pussy.

"Fuck no. Please." She stared at the ceiling as fresh tears ran down her cheeks. There was no belligerence left in her voice, only pleading as another, more forceful caress of the whip sent stabs of pain shooting upward. Her wet pussy colored the frayed end.

"You have a safeword. If you really want to stop, say it, slave. Otherwise, I will continue to ignore your ranting until you…acquiesce."

Another word hovered on his tongue, even in her haze, she knew that but for the life of her, she didn't know what it was. A tender slap of the single-tail teased her labia and she knew the next would be hard.

She was right. The sting made her grateful for the bindings that held her up and her voice cried out. "Let me wear Master Jeff's come. Please." Another blow up between her legs and her head came off the desk. Rand stood a short distance away and her eyes searched his. Only he could stop this torment and only if she begged. Her pride fizzled and she looked at him beseechingly. "Please, I can't take…please…let me…let him come on me. Please, Sir. Please. I'll do whatever you want. Just stop…please."

Rand let her ramble as two of the men took her down off the desk. She fell to her knees and Brad brought the whip over to her, holding the handle to her lips. Rand's voice floated into her consciousness. "Kiss the instrument of your correction and say thank you, slave."

Automatically, she leaned forward and placed a kiss on the handle. "Thank you, Sir. Thank you for your correction."

She could barely breathe. She gulped great big breaths of air as if she'd been underwater a very long time. In her haze she saw the man Rand called Master Jeff come up to her, his cock huge in the soft light of the room. Nearly as around as her forearm and about as long, this was clearly a man to be reckoned with. His swollen cock looked ready to burst as his hand worked the shaft.

"I love the look of those stripes across your body, slave. Marked as a sex slave ought to be marked." Master Jeff's hand furiously pumped his shaft. "Grab your heels and lean back…and beg for it."

Tears still coursed down her cheeks at how low she had come. Leaning back to expose the front of her body to him, she found herself pleading with him. "Please, Sir, please let me wear your…your gift to me."

Totally ashamed at how much of a slut she'd become, she could do nothing but kneel, commanded by the men around her, one of them spurting his cum all over her breasts, the warm liquid dripping along the stripes. But she'd agreed to this in more ways than one.

Those thoughts flew out of her head as the man's cock spit his cum onto her body. She couldn't—wouldn't—look him in the eye to see him gloating over her. Turning her face to the side, away from all of them, her chin trembled as he seemed to fount forever.

At last he groaned and stepped back, accepting the warm cloth from Underwood. Meg's shoulders sagged as she realized she wasn't done yet. Two men remained to be served. The man who'd whipped her earlier...and Rand himself.

Meg didn't move from her position as Jeff cleaned himself. Rand watched her breasts rise and fall and knew she was close to being done. They'd broken her will nearly entirely, making her not only submit but beg to submit for a man she'd come to loathe. He suspected she had no fight left in her but he needed to be sure. Nodding to Brad, who had stowed the flogger and whip back in the cupboard, Rand let her know she had more to do.

"Slave, there is still another for you to serve."

She roused a little at that, her head coming around at the sound of his voice. But she didn't look up at him and didn't take her hands from her ankles where she'd bent backward to allow Jeff to cover her breasts. Her voice was no more than a murmur of assent. "Yes Sir." He could hear the weariness, the defeat in her tone and it tore at his heart.

And yet he had to do this. Only by breaking her down could he help her rebuild. Did she understand that? Did she know how lonely she looked kneeling there? How forlorn? Did she have any idea how hard his heart beat and how much he despised himself for putting her through all this in order to fulfill her wish to get rid of all her demons?

Brad's tastes were decidedly different than Jeff's. He sat in one of the large, overstuffed leather chairs, his cock out and hard. Calling to the woman, his commands were simple, as if she were a dumb animal that needed small words. "Come, slave. Crawl." He pointed between his knees.

Still without making eye contact, she sighed, a deep exhale that seemed to shake her being as she knelt up. Seeing where he pointed, she simply leaned forward and onto all fours. She had barely started before he corrected her. "On your belly, slave."

For a moment, she wavered on two hands and a knee as her mind processed his order. Rand thought she might refuse, she might balk at this final indignity. But she didn't. Sinking down onto her stomach, her eyes barely focused, she crawled along the floor and over to his chair.

Rand knew it had to hurt. The thick rug and thicker padding underneath wouldn't protect her from the scrape of the rough wool over those fresh welts. And he'd have to have the thing cleaned of the cum she was undoubtedly rubbing into it. But even though she grimaced and sniffled as she made her way slowly over the carpet, she never paused, continuing her arduous crawl from one end of the room to the other.

He noted Ed had his cock out again, rubbing it absently as he watched the beaten-down slave move along the floor. Paul did too. In fact, his own cock twitched to see her sensuous curves sliding across the intricate pattern of the rug, the milky white of her skin marked with stripes of pink and red that matched the deep colors of the carpet. She didn't stop until her head rested between Brad's feet where he sat in the chair.

"Kneel and give me your face, slut."

The word made her shiver as she got up on all fours again, her arms visibly trembling. When she looked at the man's belly, however, Brad's voice boomed out. "My face, slut. Look me in the eye."

Rand moved where he could see her, where he could determine if Brad pushed too hard. At his sharp tone, her face turned up toward Brad's and he saw the total degradation reflected in her eyes. Without warning, Brad's cock spit forth his cum so that it landed directly on her face. Tears fell to her cheeks but she didn't move as the man in the chair came, his seemingly endless supply coating her nose and mouth and chin.

Once more Underwood was there with a cloth, his attention never diverted from the male guests. Even the butler totally ignored the shaking woman, her humiliation complete.

Everyone ignored her but Rand, however. For him she was the only one in the room, the only one he cared about. He had accepted the responsibility of taking care of her stresses this weekend and he had decided humiliation was the way to get her to break down and be honest with what she wanted out of life. Now she knelt amongst seven men, six of whom she'd serviced in some way tonight. The proof of that service dried on her skin and in her hair. She was a mess.

Ed came for a second time, hitting her in the back of the head, and she didn't turn around, only bowing her head in acceptance of what she was to them. When Paul came on her again as well, Rand watched her shoulders slowly stop shaking as she gave in entirely to their collective wills.

"Slave," he started, then realized his voice betrayed the tenderness he felt for her at this moment. "Slave," he said again, his voice louder and rougher. "We are done with you for now. Crawl to the door and kneel until you are called."

She hesitated and Rand realized she wasn't sure if she was supposed go to her belly or to her hands. "Go!" he thundered. "On all fours, crawl over to that door before you are punished for disobedience."

At the sound of his bellow she shrank down, as if afraid of him. Damn it. Why did subs always think their Masters enjoyed humiliation? He hated it. Hated what he had to do to her and hated how like an asshole he felt right now.

As if he could read the shame in Rand's face, Jeff clapped him on the shoulder. "Well, my friend, once again you've provided an excellent evening's amusement. But I must be going."

Rand turned and forced a smile he didn't feel, more for Meg's sake than his friend's, even making a joke out of what had transpired. "I'm glad you gentlemen could...come...this evening."

They chuckled and Paul spoke up. "You know, if you need help putting away your toy before we go, I don't mind helping."

Seth set down his drink and rubbed his hands together. "None of us mind helping, my boy."

Rand's grin turned genuine as he caught their drift. They were right. The perfect denouement to the public part of her ordeal. "Thank you, gentlemen. That's a very kind offer."

At Rand's nod, Underwood pushed forward a square box covered with a serviceable red tablecloth. With a flourish, he pulled the covering off to reveal a small, silver cube of a cage on wheels. Paul leaned forward and undid the clasp that held the front closed, swinging the door open wide.

Seth made a show of inspecting the cage, finally shaking his head. "Another wager, gentlemen. I say the young slut doesn't fit in that tiny space."

Rob snorted. "I'm still not sure who's won or lost the first bet. But this one is a sure thing. I'm in for a hundred says she does."

Once more the money was gathered, with Underwood as the holder until either Meg fit into the tiny cube or didn't.

They'd spoken loudly, making sure she heard how she'd become an object of money to some. Rand had bet she would fit and now he called out to her. "Come, slave. Some of my guests are anxious to lose their money."

Wearily she crawled back across the room. Not until she came nearer did the men part to let her through. Only then did she get a look at what they expected her to do.

"Inside."

Even as Rand commanded her, she shook her head. She didn't like this. None of the evening had gone as she'd expected. The last time she had been with Rand, he'd been charming and witty and a pain in the ass in all the right ways. Tonight he'd been demeaning and cruel and had pushed hard against her sense of propriety and self-worth. And now he wanted her to crawl into that thing?

"Sit on the floor of the cage and back yourself into it."

She looked up to see Ed attempting to be helpful. Clearly he'd bet she would fit. But then Jeff sneered down at her, his look just as clear that he'd bet she wouldn't. Seeing a way to get a little of her own back at the asshole, she turned, setting her rear on the floor of the cage and bending nearly double. Decidedly unhappy, Meg crawled into the cage, inch by slow inch.

In order to fit all of her inside, she had to scrunch up and lean against the thin bars, leaving no room to move, no way to turn around.

Rand now stooped before the open door of the cage. An odd look crossed his features and then was gone. But Meg didn't care. She was theirs to use as they saw fit. And if that meant being tightly squeezed into this small space, so be it. She had no strength left to argue or fight.

She'd wrapped her arms around her knees and Rand now took the cuffs at her wrists and brought them up one at a time to fasten to the corners of the cage with little brass locks. He did the same to her feet before closing the cage door, slipping a somewhat larger lock over the clasp. Meg's breath caught as she realized she was trapped.

"Ha! Told you she'd fit!" Paul and Ed grinned and accepted their share of the winnings from Underwood while Seth simply laughed and Jeff glowered. Rand, Rob and Brad also ended up a little richer as a direct result of her caging.

Now that the money had been won and lost, she expected Rand to produce the keys and let her out. She'd proven that she fit. And it was decidedly hard to breathe all bent up like a crumpled piece of paper.

In horror, she watched them take their leave of Rand, the entire party walking out the door and leaving her alone, forgotten now that she was "put away". Several of the room's small lights went out until only one burned behind her somewhere. Was Underwood still here? Becoming frantic, she tried to look around but there wasn't enough room in the cage for her to lift her head to turn it. She could only look out the side where she'd rested her head on her knees in order to fit in this small space.

"Is anyone there?"

Even to her, her voice sounded muffled by her twisted position. No one answered and she called louder. "Underwood? Are you there?"

A door snicked shut behind her and her breath caught as she realized the butler had chosen to not answer her. He had left her as deliberately as the guests, as callously as Rand had.

Desperately she tried to keep hold of her reason, even as panic lapped at the edges. Surely Rand would be back in a moment. He would do the polite thing and see his guests to the door and then come back and let her out of this infernal thing. Damn that idiot who sneered at her and who had egged her on all night with his condescending tone. If it hadn't been for him, she might have pulled the plug on this whole thing earlier. Now she was locked in and it was too late.

She pulled at the bars again as panic truly threatened. Meg had been bound in inescapable bondage more times than she could count but had never been left alone like this. Bile rose in her throat at the stench of cum that covered her body and she wanted nothing more than to be let out.

"Tell me what you are."

Rand's voice commanded her from behind. She didn't know what he meant. She tried to speak but her words came out strangled and soft as her crunched position didn't give her much breath.

"What do you mean? Rand...I..."

He stooped down to look at her and she saw a fierce light in his eyes. His gaze seemed to bore into her soul and if she could have, she would've squirmed away from it.

"Tell me what you are."

What was she? What did he mean? Stuttering a little, she grappled with the question, her voice breathless as she tried to answer. "I…I'm a buyer for Coughlin's. I'm a daughter…and I'm…I'm a submissive."

Rand shook his head with impatience. "The buyer is what you do. The daughter is simply a relationship, submissive is the role you're playing." His eyes bore into hers. "Tell me what you are."

She searched for an answer, grasping at straws as he drilled her for an answer she didn't know. "A woman?" she guessed.

"That is your gender and a part of who you are." His voice dropped to a quiet intensity. "Tell me what you are."

Meg had no idea what answer he wanted. The cramped confines of the cage made her muscles ache and she took as deep a breath as she had room for before finally admitting her ignorance. "I don't understand the question."

The disappointment on his face brought tears to her eyes. Before she could come up with another guess, Rand stood, hooking a leash through the bars of her cage. For the first time, she realized the thing had wheels as he pulled it over the carpet to the door.

"Rand…please…help me. I don't know what you want."

He didn't look back at her as he wheeled her over the bump and onto the wooden floor of the corridor. She tried to follow what rooms he pulled her in and out of dark had fallen and several of the rooms had no lights. Would she never get her bearings in this house?

Moments later she recognized the door they stood before. Above her, she heard Rand get out the key and when he pushed open the door to pull her inside, she almost breathed a sigh of relief. The dungeon was her home here. While it often meant torment, it also meant familiarity. By bringing her here, he signaled that her ordeal was almost over.

He pulled the cage until it sat beside the big bed. But he didn't let her out as she expected. Instead, he bent down again so she could see him.

"Think about what you are. And when you're ready to tell me, let me know."

She didn't like this. "I don't know what the fuck I am, can't you understand me? I don't know what you want from me."

Her anger didn't seem to faze him at all. Without another word, he simply stood and used a remote to turn down the lights to a very dim glow. In the darkness, she watched him strip off his clothes and crawl into bed naked, leaving her caged and uncomfortable.

Chapter Twelve

 හ

Rand lay nowhere near sleep. He'd turned his back on her to make her think he wasn't alert to her every sound but he registered every attempt she made to change positions and every little whimper that came out of her throat.

At first the words were only complaints and he ignored them.

"Rand, I can't move. Please…let me out of here." He heard her rattle the cage with her still-cuffed hands. "I need to stretch my legs, they're cramping up on me."

He didn't move, didn't let on he listened.

"Rand, let me out. I can't do this. Get me out of here." Her voice caught and Rand knew she was breaking.

He had made her dependent on his strength and commands for a purpose and she had accepted each of the challenges he'd thrown at her. Did she understand where he took her? That he doubted. For whatever reasons, Meg Turner trusted him far deeper than he had any right to demand. Humbled by that realization, he knew he couldn't stop now. The fact that she'd followed every step of the way meant she wanted to go to these dark places inside herself. While a part of her felt the need to at least make surface protests, that safeword hadn't come out yet and Rand lay still on the bed as Meg's voice truly began to plead.

"I don't know what I am…just tell me and then I'll know. Rand, I can't stay in here."

He stifled the chuckle. As if he would tell her the answer. In all honesty, he didn't know—only she did and she had to find it deep inside. The answers she'd given before were surface answers. She'd listed her job first, which let him know it was foremost on her mind. Her mother too. Meg might have listed her second but it was pretty obvious from some of the things she'd said that not all was well on that front.

"Come on, Rand…this isn't fun and I don't like it. Tell me what you want to hear. Whatever it is, I'll mean it. I'll be that."

She'd gone to bargaining with him. Good. Each attempt pushed her further away from civility, just as he wanted.

The other two answers she'd given hit closer to her real truth—submissive and woman. She'd said them separately and that clued him into the fact that she hadn't yet reconciled those two parts of her personality. It was very possible to be independent, proud, self-assured…and a submissive woman. A dichotomy that wasn't easy to explain and yet he'd seen it over and over.

"I can't feel my legs. They've gone numb." He heard the sniffle at the end of that fact stated as a plea. A whimper followed and Rand knew she'd moved a step closer to breaking down. He checked his watch, which he'd palmed and set next to his pillow.

"I know you can hear me, you bastard. Get me the hell out of here!"

Ah good. She'd finally gotten back to anger. Why she even bothered with the soft stuff he wasn't sure. He really thought she understood that wasn't going to work with him. Of course, the yelling wasn't going to work either but he knew she had to exhaust all the dead-end paths first.

"I hate you. You're selfish, conceited and a bully." That was followed by an extended set of rattling to the point where he almost rolled over to make sure she couldn't flip the cage and hurt herself even though he'd locked the wheels when he'd put the cage beside the bed so she wouldn't roll away. But when he didn't give her any response but a snore, she swore quietly and fell silent for a full five minutes. When she spoke again, he heard calm acceptance in her voice and he had to smile. She was textbook.

"Okay, Rand. You want me here, you want my muscles all cramped up…I accept that challenge." He listened to her breathy voice, her words coming out in the gasps of air her lungs could manage. "I'm not going to fight you anymore. I let you do things to me tonight that I…God…I have no idea why I let you do those things. But I did. And now you stick me in this cage and I can't get out…and I have no idea what you want from me. I told you what I am and you didn't like my answers. Fine. So be it. Fuck you. I'll sit here until you're ready to let me out like a good little slave girl."

He grinned. Oh she was good. Never before had he broken a woman who gave him so much fun. Meg had cores of strength inside cores of strength. Even as her body cried out in anguish, as he knew her muscles must be doing by now, she still gave him lip. He let out another snore.

"Bastard. You're not sleeping and I know it." No acrimony in her voice now, just simple statements of fact. He didn't move but didn't snore again either.

Several more minutes passed during which he heard her periodically try to shift her weight to a more bearable position. She couldn't. He knew that from experience. Everything he put her through, he'd been through as well. How could he ever understand the sub's position if he'd never been there? The training he'd been through was more extreme than he'd ever used on anyone under him. Meg, however, might push him to those extremes. She was reaching the twenty-minute mark now, long past the maximum anyone else had ever spent in that cramped little cage.

Meg's determination to accept whatever he dished out was wearing thin. Her legs had gone past the screaming stage into the burning stage and now were totally numb. Her wrists ached where he'd fastened them to the cage, the cuffs not tight, but incredibly uncomfortable. Wiggling her fingers and toes were options he'd left her and she did that periodically. Although with her numb legs, wiggling her toes only caused shoots of tingles in her calves so she stopped doing that.

She meant to sigh but it came out as a whimper when she tried to ease the strained muscles of her neck. What the hell did he want from her anyway? After getting locked in here, she hadn't really given his question much thought, having no clue what he wanted to hear. She'd given the answers she knew, then tried a couple more, thinking those were what he wanted to hear. She'd even asked him point blank what he wanted her to say so she could say it and get out. None of those approaches had worked.

She had known the fake tears early on wouldn't work but had gone through the motions anyway just on the off chance. They wouldn't have worked with Jack either. But the pleading always had. And anger had worked on the one occasion Jack had remained tough through her pleading. None of those tactics worked with Rand. Meg whimpered again as a muscle in her leg twitched and set off a wave of pins and needles.

Damn him! What did he want from her? What did he mean by "tell me what you are"? Okay, she wasn't her job, although she couldn't escape being a daughter or a woman or a submissive. So where did that leave her since he had dismissed all those?

Real tears formed in her eyes as more of her muscles twitched and cramped on her. She'd long since passed restlessness and moved fully into frustration because she couldn't stretch, couldn't move except to cause herself pain. She grabbed the bars with the tips of her fingers and shook for all she was worth, ignoring the pain to wordlessly cry out her anguish.

The stabs went deep and she sank into despair, her whimpering turning to small sobs. What was she? If she could answer that, she could get out of this mess.

Rand had truly fallen asleep this time. Between her sniffles, she listened to his soft, regular breathing and saw his shoulders under the sheet rise and fall in a steady rhythm. She would be here for hours and she had no recourse but to think and bear the pain.

What was she at the core? Silent tears fell from her closed eyes as she looked deep. In the privacy afforded her by Rand's sleeping, Meg faced truths she usually locked away.

At the core of her being lay disappointment in herself. She'd set such high goals for her life and yet she'd settled for so much less. What had happened to her dream of being a painter? Of working in oils and making her living as an artist? Somewhere along the line, the need to pay the rent became more important than her need to chase her dreams. She hadn't even picked up a brush in the past year. In the darkness of the night, locked into a tiny cage, she remembered the rainbow of her dreams and mourned their loss.

For a moment she entertained thoughts of Rand "adopting" her, becoming her patron like artists had in the old days. She imagined herself living in a small cottage on this estate, working away on the next Great Masterpiece, her every need attended to, free to do nothing but be inspired and paint.

The tears continued to fall as she recognized that for the fantasy it was. That would make her no more than a kept woman, to be tossed out whenever a new talent caught his fancy. Wasn't that the problem with the patronage system all those centuries ago?

But was she destined to remain a small cog in the retail world all the rest of her life? The rut took more and more of a toll on her spirit. How much more could she take?

Out of habit, she tried to move, the pain forcing a cry from her throat. Like a single drop that begins the river that runs to the ocean, that cry became the catalyst that provoked the flood. She sobbed in earnest, her spirit falling to the bottom of her psyche. What was she, he had asked? Pushing the dreams aside to look at the real her, she found emptiness. She was nothing.

Dimly aware that he folded back the top of the cage and lowered the sides, no strength remained in her to struggle or move. He unbound her hands but it didn't matter. His arms were around her as her soul sobbed out her frustrations and disillusionments.

Her sobs became sniffles and Rand was there with a tissue at her nose, telling her to blow as if she were a child. Meg didn't protest. That was exactly what she felt like. He wiped her eyes, then picked her up and put her into the large bed, sliding in beside her and once again pulling her into his arms.

Rand looked down at the woman he held, an unfamiliar feeling of tenderness crawling along the pathways to his heart. He'd broken women before, building them back up into stronger, more independent women. What was so different about this one?

Maybe it was her already-fierce sense of self-reliance. Or perhaps it was her incredible willingness to let him lead her along such dark paths. Or maybe it was the way her cheek dimpled when she smiled. He bent so his lips could whisper into her ear.

"Tell me what you are."

The shake of her head was barely perceptible, her voice barely audible. "I am nothing." Her voice caught at the end and Rand knew she meant it. Problem was, she was still wrong.

Normally, he put the sub back in the cage at this point until she could find an honest answer inside herself. Many of them would break before he'd reassembled the thing, finding and touching that core in a desperate attempt to remain free.

But he knew that wouldn't work for Meg. Her body sagged in exhaustion and he pulled her tighter into his embrace. She had been through a lot—the exposing of herself last night at the club, the use of her under the table and then tonight, putting her on display as a centerpiece for the food, using her breasts to serve the dishes. The flogging, the whipping, all the men's cum she still wore. And finally the caging, forcing her body into a tight space and allowing her no movement. All those things had stripped away as many layers as were going to go. He'd pushed her far more than he'd ever pushed any woman and now as she sobbed in his arms and turned to her tormentor for comfort, he found himself pulling her closer, his mouth near her ear to whisper the truth.

"What you are can be summed up in one word." He paused. "Mine."

The answer surprised them both.

The word sank through her despair to echo in the very deepest part of her psyche. "Mine." Her sobs stopped as she searched his eyes for the truth and found only caring and compassion. The last brick of her defenses fell and she reached up to give herself to him with her kisses, her lips searching for his, willingly open and giving herself to him with every part of her being. Her very soul hungered for him.

She fed him her passion and he answered her in kind. Masterful, his hands moved her body so that she lay on top of him, first cupping the cheeks of her derrière then sliding up to fondle her breasts. Tingles emanated from her skin where his fingers brushed against the welts but they only fed her hunger and she opened to him, her legs sliding down in an embrace even as her own hands slipped along his shoulders.

"Slide down on me, Meg. Bring me in."

With sudden clarity, Meg understood he spoke in metaphors as well as reality. Yes, he wanted her to take his cock into her body and she shifted her weight so that his cock slid along the wetness of her slit. The hard tip pressed against her and with a small moan, she closed her eyes and reveled in the wonderful way her pussy gaped, ready for him.

But his words held a deeper meaning. Rand wanted to be a part of her life as something more than just her Dom. He had told her she was his—all she had to do was agree. She only had to let him into her life and her submission would be complete. Opening her legs wider, she pressed her pussy against his cock even as her lips descended on his in a kiss, accepting him, needing him, wanting him.

With a thrust upward, Rand impaled her, his hands rubbing her sore skin and taking her desire even higher. Unbound, of her own free will, Meg moved with him, her body saying "yes" to him with more power than her voice could ever yield.

His hands fisted in her hair, their tongues entwined as their bodies moved in tandem. She gave him her answer, opening wider as they moved faster. Nature had them in thrall now and neither could've parted even had they wanted to.

Consumed by passion, Meg rocked in time with Rand, hardly able to breathe as his cock pounded the tattoo of their passion. The sound of their heartbeats drummed through their veins, beating faster and faster with each passing second. Meg stopped trying to analyze anything. Rand claimed her. Rand wanted her. Rand had called her "mine". Each thrust of his cock into her needy pussy repeated the mantra in her head.

And then the words changed as her mind replayed them. "I am Rand's...I want him...I belong to him." She slammed her body onto his cock, not even realizing she breathed the words aloud. Her eyes closed as their sounds reached a crescendo.

"Rand!"

"Mine!"

Meg came loudly, her body arching as she screamed his name. She heard him claim her again and knew it to be true. Crying, she gloried in the waves that rolled over her, the incredible release of all the tensions she held inside exploding outward with force. His hands pressed her against him. Instinctively she followed his movements, riding the bursts that pulsed through her body. This was where she belonged. This was what she was—Rand's. She called his name again.

And said it again, softer now as the heat slowly cooled and her head rested on his chest. His hand caressed her hair as her body twitched a time or two, holding him inside her. Her face was wet from her tears but she made no attempt to dry her cheeks. For the first time in her life, she felt sated...filled...complete.

Loath to move, Rand lay on the bed in his dungeon, a beautiful woman wrapped in his arms. A woman who, until just moments ago, was nothing more than a sub to him. Someone to play with, even if he had seen her as a bit of a challenge. He hadn't been looking for love and hadn't treated her with love. In fact, he'd been harder on her than on most subs who came to him for breaking.

But somewhere along the line, his heart discovered what his brain was only just figuring out. Meg Turner wasn't just another sub.

Underwood stood in the shadows as Rand had ordered him to earlier. Nodding to him now, Rand held Meg closer as the butler covered them both with a thick comforter before leaving them alone. Knowing he had found something unique and special, Rand drifted off to sleep, his cock still buried inside the woman he loved.

Chapter Thirteen

ℬ

With a groan and a stretch, Meg worked out the kinks, not only from the night's sleep, but from her hard use yesterday. Rand's place lay empty but still warm. Smiling, she stretched again, rolling over and nestling her body in the spot he'd vacated.

Her eyes fell on the cage, now reassembled. Had she really fit into that tiny thing? No wonder she'd hit bottom.

Sighing, she sat up, hugging her knees to her chest. But that put pressure on her breasts and she looked down, gasping at what she saw. Thin pink lines crisscrossed the white flesh, several obviously deeper than the others. Gingerly, she ran a finger over them and found the sensation wasn't at all unpleasant. They made her remember how she'd writhed for Rand's guests the night before, how she had begged to wear their cum.

Which reminded her... A further inspection showed several smears over the pink stripes on her belly. She touched her hair and found it matted in places where the dried cum stuck together. Making a face, she crawled out of the bed and headed for the bath even as her stomach growled in hunger.

The dungeon contained no clock and Meg had no idea how long she'd slept in Rand's arms. As she cleaned up, using a healthy dose of shampoo and lots and lots of soap, she thought about last night's events. But a knock on the shower door prevented her from getting very far.

"Fresh towels for you on the sink, miss."

"Thank you, Underwood." Funny how accustomed she'd become to the butler's silent entries.

"And breakfast's ready for you in the room."

"Thank you. I won't be long."

"Take your time, miss."

The door shut and Meg hurried through the rest of her shower as her stomach growled again. The scent of bacon wafted in with the butler, making her realize just how long it had been since she had eaten.

She toweled off with the large, fluffy white towels he'd brought in, taking a moment to quickly run a comb through her hair. But with all the tangles brought on by last night's activities, she found several rat's nests that needed to be worked out with her fingers first. Finally satisfied that she'd found most of them, she wrapped a towel around her more for warmth than any other reason and headed back into the dungeon.

A table had been set up near the bed, a white tablecloth laid over it with place settings and chairs for two. Underwood stood at ease beside the table, holding her chair for her. Smiling, Meg allowed him to help her sit. He had barely pushed the chair under the table when Rand came in.

Meg's breath caught to see him, dressed in a blue oxford shirt with his sleeves rolled up and jeans that had seen better days. His hair, still damp from his shower, clung to his temples and Meg's heart beat a little harder.

"Thank you, Underwood. That will be all."

The butler gave a small bow and departed as Rand took the seat opposite her. With grace, he lifted a lid and Meg's nose was assailed by the wonderful scents of cinnamon and maple.

"French toast?"

"Thank you, I'd love a slice or two."

With a twinkle in his eyes, Rand lifted two slices of thick bread, neatly fried to a golden brown and dripping with butter, and set them on her plate. Small cruets of various syrups sat neatly in a small carrier and Meg chose the one labeled Vermont Maple and poured a generous amount over her toast.

"Are you hiding your marks from me?"

Meg looked up in surprise but the grin on his face as he helped himself to the bacon gave away the fact that he teased her.

"No." She shook her head. "The room's cold."

"I can always warm your skin for you."

Meg laughed outright when he wiggled his eyebrows and jerked his head toward the bed.

"Much as I'd like that, my dear Sir, I think I'll eat breakfast instead." As if to emphasize her point, her stomach rumbled loudly.

"Another county heard from." Rand took the maple syrup and poured an equally generous amount over his own toast and bacon. But when he set it back down, his eyes were more serious. "Meg…" he started, his voice trailing off as if he weren't sure where to start.

Meg looked up from her breakfast, a bite of cinnamon French toast melting in her mouth. She waited for him to go on, prompting him when he didn't. "Yes?"

"I'd like to see your breasts."

Relatively sure that wasn't what he'd started to say to her, she put her fork down and pulled the towel open. Deliberately pushing her chair back, she stood, stepping around the table so he could see the pink marks that covered her. His hand on her skin as he ran his palm along them felt warm and inviting.

Rand nodded. "They look good. How do they feel?" He patted her hip and she went back to her chair, draping the towel over her shoulders to keep off the chill.

"Actually, they pull a little, but unless they're touched, I really hardly know they're there."

Rand smiled and she saw the devil in his eyes that always meant mischief. "Wait until you put your clothes on."

She laughed, taking another bite of breakfast.

For several minutes they ate in companionable silence. But something hung in the air until Meg decided she might as well address it. "Rand..." Now it was her turn to hesitate as she formed the thought in her head.

"Yes?"

"Last night, in the cage...I told you I was nothing..." Her cheeks blushed a bright pink at the admission. Here in the light of a new day, nothing seemed as bleak as it had last night. And yet there was no sense denying she'd hit bottom.

He didn't say anything, giving her the time she needed.

"I am something, you know. I just didn't find it last night." She held up a hand to stave off his interruption. "I know, you said I was yours. And I am...in a lot of ways. I mean, I am yours for the weekend, just not yours...forever. I don't belong to you. I belong to myself. However," she held up a hand again as if Rand had made a move to speak, even though he hadn't. "However, you were right in saying that I was wrong in saying I'm nothing. What I meant then was...that..."

She trailed off, her train of thought derailing, not with a fiery crash but with a whimper, a puff of inanity clouding what she meant.

Rand just sat, waiting for her to finish. And when it became obvious she was done, he leaned forward, staring at her intently. "You want to try again?"

Meg sighed and nodded, putting down the fork she'd been waving around. She folded her hands neatly on her lap and gave it another go.

"I'm not nothing. I know I said that last night but I wanted you to know I have a little more self-esteem than that." She dropped her eyes and looked around the table, as if the words she wanted were hidden behind the salt shaker or under the dish of butter. Giving up, she leaned back in her chair, her appetite suddenly gone. "I am

...something....someone. I just haven't found out what or who."

"What or who do you want to be?"

So wrapped in her own thoughts, she missed the timbre of tension in his voice. He still sat forward, his elbows on the table, his gaze fixed on her.

"You promise you won't laugh?"

"Meg, I would never, ever laugh at you."

She looked up at that, seeing the total seriousness in his eyes. Feeling almost ashamed that she'd even asked that question, she nodded. "Thank you for that. And I know you won't. It's just that..."

"That so many others have?"

She nodded, feeling a tickle in her nose, warning her that tears were close. Clearing her throat and taking a bite of toast to banish them, she took the plunge.

"Okay. What I really want to be? Really, deep down inside?" She smiled self-consciously as she made her admission, feeling a bit like an awkward schoolgirl confessing she wanted to be an actress, just like every other little girl. "Deep down inside, I want to be a painter and a writer. I want to write children's books and illustrate them myself."

He sat back, perplexed. "Now why would I laugh at a wonderful desire like that?"

Meg's grin, wry and humorless, twisted her face. "Because it isn't practical. It's not going to make me enough money to live on and I'm just not that talented." She hadn't meant to make the last sound as bitter as it did.

"Whose words are those? 'Cause they're certainly not yours."

She shook her head. "The first two reasons are my mother's...and much as I hate to admit it, she's right. Writing children's books and doing the illustrations isn't a fulltime career that pays the bills. The last? About not being talented enough? Comes from my advisor at college who pretty much told me I'd never be anything more than a second-rate artist."

"The man deserves to be fired."

She missed the anger in his voice. "No, he did me a favor. I never won any great scholarships on my art pieces, never won any awards. I'm good. I'm not great. And great is what gets you the big prizes."

Meg looked over at him, catching a glimpse of—something—before he leaned back and crossed his arms. What was going on in that dominant brain of his? She narrowed her eyes and tried to figure it out but his next question sent her mind in an entirely different direction.

"And who do you want to be?"

Although tempted to laugh at the sudden change, Meg smiled and sat back. "I want to be a person who is a good friend, who is pleasant to be around, cheerful...and satisfied with her life."

"But you're not satisfied now?"

Meg shook her head, memories of her darkest moments coming to mind. She thought of the store and the clothes and felt her stomach roil. "No, I'm not satisfied with either who I am or what I am doing with my life."

"And what are you going to do to change it?"

She looked at him with exasperation. "I have no idea, that's the problem. I don't hate my job but I don't love it either. And I can't quit because, much as she wants me to, I'm not running home to mama. There are bills to be paid, school loans to finish off..."

She trailed off, shaking her head.

"And what about me?"

Meg looked up in confusion. "What about you?"

"Do you remember what I called you last night?"

Her cheeks colored. "Yes."

"What does that mean to you?"

191

"I think the operative question here, is — what does that mean to *you*, Rand. You're the one who said it and, like I said, I know I'm yours for the weekend but..."

"But I didn't mean only for the weekend, last night."

"Well, I guess that's what I'm asking. What did you mean by it?"

He didn't answer for a long time and Meg wondered if she'd crossed an invisible line. Finally he stood, pushing away the uneaten remains of his breakfast. As hungry as she'd been earlier, she stood as well, the towel slipping from her shoulders, her appetite nonexistent.

"I'll send Underwood for the dishes."

Without another word, he turned and left the room, leaving Meg behind, her mouth open and her brow furrowed.

Completely confused by him, Meg took the towel back to the bath, then came and sat on the edge of the bed, trying to figure out what had just happened.

When Underwood came in, she still sat there, cross-legged on the bed, idly toying with her breasts, part of her mind identifying and registering the various levels of soreness depending on where she rubbed and how hard. But most of her mind toyed with Rand's confusing statement. "But I didn't mean only for the weekend, last night."

Did that mean he wanted her here permanently? As in 24/7? Or did it mean he wanted to start dating? Or did it mean he didn't mean the weekend, last night...but he did this morning? Many things were said in the heat of lovemaking that were regretted in the morning. Did he regret saying that to her? He shouldn't. While it had provided comfort last night, Meg understood her role as bottom to his Top. He was her Dom, she was his submissive. She wouldn't press him for more...or did he want her to?

Underwood's entrance interrupted her reverie. "Good morning again, miss."

"Good morning, Underwood."

"Note from Master Rand for you here." He handed her a long, white envelope labeled in his masculine scrawl. At least he'd written "Slave" across the front and not her name. She took that as a good sign as she slid out the note inside.

Slave,

Give your mouth to Underwood and when he's done, he will clear the dishes.

Remember, you are nothing more than a slave in this household, to be used as I see fit and by whom I see fit.

Rand

She looked at Underwood, her eyes narrowing in suspicion. When he pulled a pillow off the bed and placed it on the floor in front of him, then simply pointed to it, her suspicions were confirmed.

Meg debated. She could say no any time she wanted. Rand had assured her that her safeties were in effect this weekend, although he'd been hesitant about giving that to her. And she'd already given this guy a blowjob. Did they really expect her to give him another?

But the butler already had his cock out, his hand absently running along its length as she folded the note and dropped it on the bed before coming to kneel before him.

"I don't do this for just anybody, you know," she told him as she took his cock in her hand.

"Of course you don't, miss. You serve your Master…as do I."

She opened her mouth to ask him what he meant but he pressed forward, his cock at her lips. Obediently, she opened for him, running her tongue over the stretched skin, almost in relief. While Rand was currently confusing the hell out of her, Underwood's directness had an incredible calming effect. One could always count on him to be detached and professional.

And so could she. Smiling, she bent to her task, kind of enjoying the fact that the two of them, so obviously servants of the Great Rand Arthur, were going at it at his direction. There was something perverse about it—wonderfully perverse. Her smile became a grin as she gave the older butler the best blowjob she'd ever given anyone. Ever.

Underwood's thrusts into the depths of her throat became stronger as he came closer to coming. Meg pulled back, wanting to give him the ultimate gift. "Underwood," she gasped, not wanting to leave his cock alone too long. "Come in my mouth. Let me swallow you."

"As you will, miss."

She wrapped her lips around him again and pressed forward until her nose was buried in his groin. His hand on her head guided her to his needs and seconds later, she felt the hot liquid fill her mouth and slide down her throat. Pulling back only a little, she struggled to swallow as he kept coming, filling her as quickly as she could swallow it down.

But at last the butler slowed and Meg took the opportunity to slide her tongue all around his softening cock, cleaning it of every drop of cum.

"Thank you, miss."

Was the butler's voice just a little breathy? With a grin, Meg leaned back on her heels. "I'm glad to be of service, Mr. Underwood."

The older man grinned uncharacteristically as he tucked his cock back inside his briefs and closed his pants. "You do Master Rand proud, miss."

Meg blushed with pleasure as the butler put the two chairs along the wall and wheeled the table out the room's service door to the kitchen. Meg smiled and went to sit on the bed again, picking up the note and mulling over just what it might be that Rand wanted from her.

Chapter Fourteen

∞

Rand took his frustrations out on his golf swing. After writing the note and deliberately attempting to make Meg run, he'd gone out on the back veranda and paced for nearly ten minutes. Unable to stand still, he'd grabbed a driver he'd been trying out earlier in the week, pocketed a dozen balls and walked to his back lawn where it stretched for nearly two acres of mown perfection. The first ball he'd slammed into the woods on the right that bordered the property. The second had gone wild, landing in the swimming pool, also to his right. The third shot went straighter, landing square in the fountain that served as a centerpiece for the lawn.

He lined up his fourth shot, thinking that if he tried hard enough, maybe he could knock the cute little cupid right off his idiotic perch on top of the fountain. But before he could swing, a movement out of the corner of his eye disrupted his concentration. Underwood stood a little way off, looking calmer and more composed than usual.

"Don't tell me..."

"Yes sir. She has a very fine mouth."

Rand nearly threw the club to the ground. "Damn her! I have pushed and prodded, I have demeaned her in front of others, I've treated her like a slave and given her away to you—twice! What the hell am I going to do with her?"

"Do you wish an answer, sir? Or was that rhetorical?"

Rand looked at his butler but saw no amusement in the man's eyes. "If I didn't know you better, Underwood, I'd think you were making fun of me."

"Never, sir. Shall I retrieve the golf ball from the pool for you?"

"You *are* making fun of me."

"Of course I am, sir."

This time the twinkle sparkled in the butler's eyes and Rand shook his head, chuckling. "Underwood..." He stopped, then gave a long sigh.

"Yes sir?"

"I just don't know. Is she...?" Rand let the sentence trail, unsure if he really wanted to ask the question.

Underwood simply nodded and answered him anyway. "Yes sir. She is."

With brisk efficiency, the butler turned him toward the house and gave him a little push. "Go and tell her so."

"Yes sir, Mr. Underwood." Feeling like a recalcitrant little boy, Rand faced the truth. Somewhere between the whippings and the floggings, he had fallen in love with Meg Turner and the words he'd spoken last night were from his heart. Trying to figure out the best approach to tell her that, he marched toward the house as if he marched toward his doom.

By the time he reached the door to the dungeon, he still didn't have any more of an idea how to tell her he'd fallen in love with her than he'd had when slamming the golf balls around his property. As he slid the key into the lock, another thought stopped him. What if she didn't love him back? Wasn't that part of what she had been babbling about earlier? Or had that been mere waffling because she hadn't wanted to admit her creative side to him?

Almost of its own volition, his hand turned the key. The sound of the lock giving way made him jump as he realized he'd taken the step. Squaring his shoulders, he put on his Dom persona and marched into the room as if he knew exactly what he was doing.

She sat cross-legged on the bed, her arms extended upward as if she reached for something he couldn't see. Gently twisting herself to one side, then the other, he realized she worked the muscles in her back, stretching them after all the use he'd put her though. Faint lines of pinked skin marked her breasts and stomach but they didn't temper her movements. Deliberately, he moved into her line of vision, pleased by the little start and sudden smile she gave as soon as she saw him.

"Sorry…didn't see you come in." She scrambled off the bed, dropping a pillow to the floor and kneeling on it in one swift movement. Placing her hands behind her head, she arched her back a little and presented her breasts for his inspection.

Rand raised an eyebrow. "We never did discuss protocols, did we? And now it's nearly time for you to leave."

Meg looked up at him with something close to alarm in her eyes. "Already? Seems like the day's just starting."

"It's nearly one and I'm sure you have things to do before going to work tomorrow."

At the mention of work, a shadow passed over her face. He hated that shadow. She had admitted she didn't like her job and only kept it for the money. But Rand was relatively sure she wasn't digging at him for money with that confession. Even now her jaw set and she raised her chin as she faced her responsibilities.

"Yes, now that you mention it, I do have some…things…to do before tomorrow morning." She dropped her hands to her sides and started to rise with obvious reluctance.

"Stay, slave."

A smile played on her lips as she put her knee back on the pillow and slowly relocked her fingers behind her head.

Her instant submissiveness was too much. He muttered an epithet. "Okay, stop. This is too much. Get dressed. I'll talk to you…later."

He stalked out the door, wishing for once he'd made it slamable. Damn the woman! She knelt there, with those huge doe eyes, looking so trusting. He wanted to grab the flogger and beat her skin red for what she did to him. He'd worked so hard for her trust, how could he destroy it now by telling her he wanted to break their agreement? That he wanted her as far more than just a submissive to while away the time with?

Damn Jack. Some friend he'd turned out to be. Saddling him with a woman he'd fall in love with. Next time he got the man in front of him, he just might take a flogger to him too.

Rand stalked to the library but immediately images of last night came flooding back. Meg tied and whipped while he ached to touch her. Meg begging to be covered in cum as he witnessed her incredible acts of submission and passion.

The dining room was no better and he passed it by, heading for his study. Once there, he tried not to look at the couch where he'd held her in his arms and they'd spoken as equals or at his desk where she'd crouched and suckled him at his command.

Nor was there respite on the patio, where he'd turned the hose on her Friday night, the cold water designed to break down some of her barriers. Well, he'd managed to do that all right. Problem was, he'd broken down his own at the same time.

Meg watched him go, entirely mystified at Rand's sudden outburst. What the hell had gotten into him?

"Dressed, he says. Get dressed." She stood, pursing her lips and looking around the dungeon. "Like I have a clue where my clothes might be." With a sudden blush, she remembered the clothes she'd worn out on Friday night—the mini skirt and the too-tight blouse, both covered in cum. She grinned. Knowing Underwood, they would be washed, pressed and folded neatly somewhere sensible.

"The bathroom." Snapping her fingers, she opened the door and peeked into the tiled room. Sure enough, her skirt and blouse sat neatly on the counter. Meg slipped them on, blushing again as she saw herself in the mirror. Neither piece left much to anyone's imagination.

The service door to the kitchen was ajar when she reentered the dungeon but she saw no sign of the ubiquitous butler. She wandered around the room for a bit, pausing to rest her hand on the cage that had caused her so much grief the night before. She smiled, feeling so much better about everything. While thoughts of having to go to work tomorrow still made her stomach clench, Meg felt more clearheaded than she had in a long time. She made a note to send Jack a nice bottle of wine when he returned to the States.

Although she'd poked her head through the open door to the kitchen's passageway several times in her tours around the dungeon, she didn't leave the room since Rand's last instructions weren't clear. But after half an hour, Rand still hadn't returned and the day was getting on. Like it or not, she had a life to get back to. She walked through the passage and pushed open the swinging door to the inviting kitchen.

"Hello, miss." Underwood stood at the butcher-block table, setting up a tea tray with a small pot of tea and a single cup. A few cookies on a china plate sat beside the silver tray.

"Hello, Underwood. Have you seen Rand? I mean, Mr. Arthur? He said he was coming back but he hasn't." She tried not to look at the heavy wooden table and remember being "arranged" on it. Had it been only fourteen hours ago?

"Yes, miss. He's in his study, fuming."

"Fuming?"

"Yes, miss. He's quite upset." The butler moved the cookies to the tray, then stepped to the cupboard, pulling out a tin of teabags.

"Upset? At what? Did I do something wrong?" Meg thought back through their confusing conversation at breakfast and then his strange behavior when he'd returned.

Underwood smiled and Meg narrowed her eyes at the man. In all the times she'd seen him, he'd never shown the slightest bit of devilry in him and yet a decidedly wicked gleam glinted in the butler's eyes right now.

"No, miss, you did everything right."

"Okay, Underwood...give. What's going on that I'm missing?"

"Oh miss, that would definitely not be for me to give away." The butler lifted the tray and turned to her, holding it out for her to take. "You'll find Mr. Arthur down through that hall," he paused to nod to the far door, "sulking in his study."

Automatically, Meg took the tray. "You want me to..."

"Yes, miss."

She could swear that he rocked on his heels in glee. Shaking her head, she turned to the door. "I don't know what you have up your sleeve, my dear Mr. Underwood, but I'll go along with it."

"Thank you, miss. You won't be sorry."

He held the door open for her and Meg watched the tray, careful not to tip it and slide the cookies from their plate or hot water from the teapot. She passed through the dining room, pleased to see that a curtain had been drawn over the large painting on the wall. There was a time and place for everything and right now, she wanted to get at the bottom of whatever had set Rand off.

Thankfully the door to the study wasn't closed all the way. She had no idea how Underwood balanced a tray and turned a doorknob at the same time. Pushing her foot against the study door to swing it wide, she went in with Rand's tea and cookies.

Rand stood behind his desk, looking out the long windows at the yard beyond. His back to her, he didn't turn around as she quietly came in and searched for a place to set down the tray that became heavier by the minute.

"Underwood, I tried to tell her. But it isn't fair to her. I'd be changing the rules and that isn't right. And I'm not sure I even really want to change them."

Meg opened her mouth and closed it again, throwing a glance at the open door. Maybe she could sneak out and he'd never realize…

He turned around and her chance evaporated. To cover, she tossed her head and cleared her throat. "Underwood asked me to bring you your tea before I—" *Left* was the word on her tongue but that wasn't the truth. She didn't want to leave and even if she did, she had no way home.

Rand nodded at the unspoken word and his shoulders drooped. "Thank you." He made no move from where he stood and Meg set the tray down on his paper-strewn desk with more of a clatter than she intended. Her heart beat so loudly in her own ears! The reality of what he'd spoken, which she hadn't been meant to hear, sank in.

"So what is it that isn't fair to me?" Although she trembled inside, she kept her chin steady, even though she had to rest her fingertips on his desk to keep her hands from shaking.

"I'm sorry, Meg. I thought you were…"

"I know who you thought I was. What isn't fair to me?" An edge had crept into her voice.

"Shit." Rand turned away.

"I gave you everything you asked for, met every challenge you threw at me this weekend. You stripped me of every pretense I had, broke down every wall I'd built and made me face parts of myself I'd been running away from. I let you display me to your friends. I let you give me to your friends for their use. So I think I have a right to know just what the hell you're talking about."

Her anger grew by the moment. If he intended to dump her as a submissive, she had to know now. The fantasies she'd entertained about being Rand's kept woman flashed through her head and even though she understood them for what they were, she couldn't deny her heart desperately wanted to stay with him.

"You do. You absolutely do." Rand came around the end of the desk then, taking Meg's shoulders and leading her to the couch. "Please, sit down."

Stiffly, Meg sat at one end, a little relieved when he sat beside her. But he made no further move to touch her, sitting instead facing front, his hands clasped and his elbows on his knees. Silent for several moments, Meg tried to find the patience inside her to wait without speaking or making accusations, no matter how many ran through her brain. Would he tell her thanks, but no thanks? He'd used her for his own sexual pleasure but now, after a weekend of enjoying her body and playing with her mind, he was done with her? If that was the road they were going to go down... Her anger bubbled up again.

But before she could let it out, Rand spoke and his words took the wind right out of her sails.

"Meg, you carry around a pretty healthy dose of stress and you told me you see these sessions as a way to relieve that stress. It works that way for me too. There's nothing like giving a good flogging to get out the frustrations." He grinned wryly but continued without looking at her. "When the stress comes back as quickly as I saw it happen with you, I knew I needed to get down to root causes. All the sessions you'd been doing with Jack had treated symptoms, not the actual causes of the stress.

"So I designed this weekend to do exactly that. I do a lot of work with data..." He swung his hand around in a wide gesture that took in the array of paperwork spread throughout the room. "And finding the root cause of a problem is one of the things I do best. Find the root, fix the root and the problem solves itself."

He fell silent and Meg tried to talk around the lump of emotion stuck in her throat. When she spoke, her voice was tight. "So that's what you did with me. You found the root last night. I don't like where my life is right now, either with my job or my relationship with my mother..." She swallowed hard. "But you can't fix the root. Only I can do that, is that what you're telling me? You're sending me back to the real world on my own to fix what I need to fix."

Rand finally turned to face her, a searching look in his eyes. For a moment, she thought he was going to say something but then he stood and crossed the room to his desk as if he'd made a decision. "Yes, Meg, that's exactly what I'm doing. Only you can decide if you want real change in your life. I can't do that for you."

She stood, her movements slow and controlled as she held tightly to every emotion she had that threatened to erupt. "Thank you. I appreciate your time and effort. I will work on making the changes I need to make and if you'd like, will keep you apprised of my success. I..." Her voice trailed off as she realized she really didn't have anything further to say except one thing. "Goodbye, Rand."

Turning, she walked out of the study, somehow making it calmly along the hall and into the foyer. The large front door loomed before her and she hesitated. Nothing here belonged to her and she had no ride back to her apartment. It didn't matter. She wasn't helpless.

Setting her shoulders, she opened the front door and walked out.

Underwood watched her exit into the afternoon sunshine, then glided into the study. Once again, Rand stood at the windows, staring out at nothing in particular.

"If you'll forgive my saying so, sir, you are a fool." He picked up the untouched tray.

"I forgive you. You're only stating the truth."

"Yes sir. You do know she's currently walking down the drive, with the intent to walk back to the city."

Rand turned to look at his unflappable butler, a sad smile on his face. "She's just mad enough at me to do it too."

Underwood walked to the door. "How far do you intend to let her get before you go after her, sir?"

"I am going to go after her, aren't I, Underwood."

"Yes sir, you are." When Rand didn't immediately move, Underwood prodded again. "It all depends on just how angry you want her to be at you, sir."

Rand nodded, understanding the butler's meaning. The farther Meg got, the more hurt she'd feel and the more angry she'd become. He grabbed his keys from the drawer and rushed out past his wise servant, not seeing the smile on Underwood's face, nor the wily glint in his eyes.

Rand dashed out the front door, pausing to search along the long drive for any sign of the woman he loved, catching sight of her almost to the gate at the road. How did she manage to get so far so fast? She must be furious at him at the pace she kept.

Not that he blamed her. He dashed down the steps.

"Sir!"

Rand turned at the sound of his butler's voice and caught the keys Underwood threw at him.

"Take the four-wheeler, sir."

He looked around and saw the all-terrain vehicle Underwood often used to get around the property currently parked at the side of the drive. With a wave to his butler's foresight, Rand hopped on, started it up and turned it around to head down the driveway to the woman he realized he didn't want to let get away.

Meg was already through the gates, standing at the end of his drive in seeming indecision. But even as he pulled up behind her, Rand understood the momentary confusion had nothing to do with what she did but rather where she went. She didn't seem surprised to see him, even if her eyebrow arched at the vehicle he'd rode to catch up with her.

"Meg…"

"I can't remember which way to go to get back to Route 96. Once I'm on 96 I know my way home, but did we take a right or a left to get in here? I can't remember and I've even driven this!"

Rand turned off the loud engine and crossed the space, catching her as she turned away from him and took some steps in the wrong direction. "Meg…"

He stepped in front of her, holding her in his arms. To his surprise, she didn't fight him. Her hair had slipped down to cover her face and when he brushed it back, he hid his amazement. Her face was red and puffy and still wet from her tears.

"I don't want you to go, Meg."

"What is it you want, Rand? You have me so confused about everything. I don't know what to think anymore."

"I know. That's my fault. I pushed you to face reality, then I…"

"Then you dropped me. You told me I was on my own." She looked up at him, her eyes wide and searching. "Please tell me…tell me…"

Her voice faltered and Rand understood she was scared to ask the question. He pulled her tighter.

"You are not on your own, Meg. I was wrong to say that, wrong to let you walk out. What I said last night in the heat of the moment has forced me to do a lot of thinking this morning."

Her eyes, wide and trusting, looked at him with a yearning that echoed in his own soul. He told her the truth.

"You are mine, Meg. I don't want you to go. I love you."

"You what?" She pushed away from him, her eyes searching his.

"I love you." He held up a hand, much as she had at breakfast, to stop a protest that wasn't really there. "I know, this breaks our agreement. You agreed to be my sub and I'm asking for more. If you want to walk away, I fully understand."

His voice dropped and he pulled her closer.

"But I don't want you to walk away. You took every challenge I threw at you and you not only did it but did it with such a style and grace…" Rand shook his head. "Please don't go."

"I don't want to go."

Rand sensed hesitation in her voice. "You don't want to go but…"

"But I have to."

"Why? Stay here with me."

"And be what? Your slave? Your mistress?" She shook her head but made no move away from him.

"As my wife."

Now she did push herself away. "What are you talking about? Rand, we hardly know each other. And I can't be your wife, not after…not after last night."

"What do you mean, after last night?" He knew enough not to hold her tightly right now, letting her take a few steps away as she made her argument.

She tried to explain. "Rand, those men last night saw me as your slave. I performed for them. They used me to jerk off to. If we marry and I'm your wife, those same men will see me at functions and you'll have to put up with their smirks and knowing winks. They'll make sly comments and even if they don't… It doesn't matter. You shared me with them and they'll think that gives them…privileges."

Rand shook his head. "No. That won't happen. You said you don't know me well. I hope you know me well enough to know I would never give you to the type of man you describe."

Meg's head reeled. The fantasy of being a kept woman, of having Rand as her rich patron who gave her the opportunity to paint and write, flashed through her imagination. Could it come true? Did she really want it to? Her independent streak came to the fore.

"Rand, I'm not... I don't know that I'm ready for..." Her voice trailed off at the look of disappointment in his eyes.

"I understand, Meg. I really do. I don't want to lose you. I just felt you needed to know I've broken our agreement. My heart has gotten involved."

A flood of relief made her smile. "You haven't broken any agreement I wouldn't have broken myself, Rand."

He looked at her with hope and she nodded. "Somewhere between the blowjobs to Underwood and the incessant challenges, I fell in love with you too. But I didn't know...how to deal with that in the face of so many other things you made me tackle."

"Like the fact that you don't enjoy your job and your mother drives you nuts."

She laughed outright and felt a huge weight drop from her shoulders. "Like the fact that I don't enjoy my job and my mother drives me nuts." Somehow having someone to share those frustrations with made them so much easier to handle.

"Meg, I want you to move in here and be with me twenty-four/seven." He held up his hand again to prevent her from interrupting. "But I also know that's not going to happen right now. You have things to deal with in your life." Rand pulled her close. "But you aren't alone in them. I can help you find a publisher for that children's book. And if your mother met me, she just might get off your case about remaining single."

He grinned and Meg loved the single dimple that appeared in his cheek. "When my mother meets you, don't be surprised if she goes off screaming into the night."

Now he laughed outright as he turned her toward the four-wheeler. "Come on, let's head back to the house and have a decent lunch, since neither of us ate much earlier." He helped her onto the seat, enjoying the fact that all she wore was the short skirt and the skimpy top. "And later I'll take you home in style." He revved the engine and shouted over it. "The future we'll handle as it comes."

Meg put her arms around his waist and lay her cheek on his strong back. Somehow, having someone to lean against felt awfully comfortable. And her problems suddenly seemed surmountable rather than interminable. Grinning as he sped up the driveway, Meg decided she needed to send Jack a huge bouquet of roses along with that bottle of wine.

Epilogue

ॐ

The whip fell across soft white shoulders that had never done hard lifting or heavy labor. These were shoulders used by friends to cry on, shoulders that pushed nothing stronger than a paintbrush, although they did lift heavy canvasses, setting the easel so she could catch the best rays of the sun. The whip slashed bright pain in a straight line across her skin and she hung her head so that her long hair hid her smile.

A third and a fourth welt rose to meet the first two and her voice cried out in answer to the whip's crack. The whip snapped one last time before he set it aside, coming behind her to rest his cool hands on her burning shoulders. She let her head fall forward and her knees weaken, enjoying the sexual arousal his touch always produced. And when he brushed the hair from her face and she lifted her gaze to his, her smile showed her deep satisfaction and contentment.

Also by Diana Hunter

ഌ

eBooks:

About the Author

മ

For many years, Diana Hunter confined herself to mainstream writings. Her interest in the world of dominance and submission, dormant for years, bloomed when she met a man who was willing to let her explore the submissive side of her personality. In her academic approach to learning about the lifestyle, she discovered hundreds of short stories that existed on the topic, but none of them seemed to express her view of a d/s relationship. Challenged by a friend to write a better one, she wrote her first BDSM novel, Secret Submission, published by Ellora's Cave Publishing.

Diana Hunter welcomes comments from readers. You can find her website and email address on her author bio page at www.ellorascave.com.

Tell Us What You Think

We appreciate hearing reader opinions about our books. You can email us at Comments@EllorasCave.com.

Why an electronic book?

We live in the Information Age—an exciting time in the history of human civilization, in which technology rules supreme and continues to progress in leaps and bounds every minute of every day. For a multitude of reasons, more and more avid literary fans are opting to purchase e-books instead of paper books. The question from those not yet initiated into the world of electronic reading is simply: *Why?*

1. *Price.* An electronic title at Ellora's Cave Publishing and Cerridwen Press runs anywhere from 40% to 75% less than the cover price of the exact same title in paperback format. Why? Basic mathematics and cost. It is less expensive to publish an e-book (no paper and printing, no warehousing and shipping) than it is to publish a paperback, so the savings are passed along to the consumer.

2. *Space.* Running out of room in your house for your books? That is one worry you will never have with electronic books. For a low one-time cost, you can purchase a handheld device specifically designed for e-reading. Many e-readers have large, convenient screens for viewing. Better yet, hundreds of titles can be stored within your new library—on a single microchip. There are a variety of e-readers from different manufacturers. You can also read e-books on your PC or laptop computer. (Please note that Ellora's Cave does not endorse any specific brands.

You can check our websites at www.ellorascave.com or www.cerridwenpress.com for information we make available to new consumers.)

3. *Mobility.* Because your new e-library consists of only a microchip within a small, easily transportable e-reader, your entire cache of books can be taken with you wherever you go.

4. *Personal Viewing Preferences.* Are the words you are currently reading too small? Too large? Too… ANNOYING? Paperback books cannot be modified according to personal preferences, but e-books can.

5. *Instant Gratification.* Is it the middle of the night and all the bookstores near you are closed? Are you tired of waiting days, sometimes weeks, for bookstores to ship the novels you bought? Ellora's Cave Publishing sells instantaneous downloads twenty-four hours a day, seven days a week, every day of the year. Our webstore is never closed. Our e-book delivery system is 100% automated, meaning your order is filled as soon as you pay for it.

Those are a few of the top reasons why electronic books are replacing paperbacks for many avid readers.

As always, Ellora's Cave and Cerridwen Press welcome your questions and comments. We invite you to email us at Comments@ellorascave.com or write to us directly at Ellora's Cave Publishing Inc., 1056 Home Avenue, Akron, OH 44310-3502.

COMING TO A BOOKSTORE NEAR YOU!

ELLORA'S CAVE

Bestselling Authors Tour

UPDATES AVAILABLE AT
WWW.ELLORASCAVE.COM

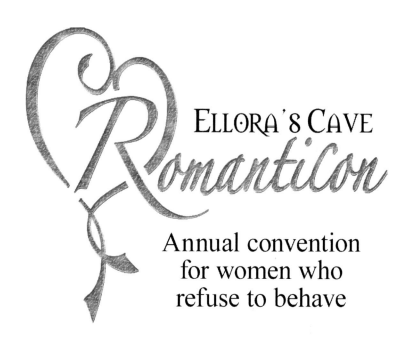

ELLORA'S CAVE
Romanticon

Annual convention
for women who
refuse to behave

COLUMBUS DAY WEEKEND

www.JasmineJade.com/Romanticon
For additional info contact: conventions@ellorascave.com

Discover for yourself why readers can't get enough of the multiple award-winning publisher

Ellora's Cave.

Whether you prefer e-books or paperbacks,

be sure to visit EC on the web at
www.ellorascave.com

for an erotic reading experience that will leave you breathless.

Breinigsville, PA USA
22 November 2010
249863BV00001B/104/P